MANSFIELD PARK REVISITED

MANSFIELD PARK REVISITED

Merryn Williams

© Merryn Williams, 2019

Published by Plas Gwyn books

A CIP catalogue record for this book is available from the British Library.

ISBN 978-0-9533952-3-1

Book layout and design by Clare Brayshaw

Prepared and printed by:

York Publishing Services Ltd
64 Hallfield Road
Layerthorpe
York YO31 7ZQ

Tel: 01904 431213

Website: www.yps-publishing.co.uk

Contents

The Characters

Sir Thomas Bertram, Member of Parliament, owner of
Mansfield Park
Lady Bertram, his wife
Tom
Edmund (Eddy)
Maria,
Julia – their children
Mrs. Desiree Norris, Lady Bertram's elder sister
Mrs. Frances Price, Lady Bertram's younger sister
Franny Price, her daughter
William, Susie, Sam and Charles, Franny's siblings
Reverend Doctor Theodore Grant, the vicar of Mansfield
Mrs. Gillian Grant, his wife
Henry Crawford, her half-brother
Mary Crawford (Missy), her half-sister
James Rushworth (Rush), Maria's fiancé, later husband
Mrs. Elizabeth Rushworth, his mother
The Honourable John Yates, Tom's friend.

And also
Gabriela, the Bertrams' maid
Joey, a friend of Mrs. Price.

*The characters are Jane Austen's. But the interpretation is
mine.*

1

Sir Thomas and Lady Bertram

About thirty years ago, Miss Maria Ward, of Huntingdon, had the good luck to meet Sir Thomas Bertram, the member for Mid-Northamptonshire, at a Young Conservative dance. They liked each other immediately and nine months later were married. Sir Thomas had inherited his seat from his late father and hoped, when the time came, to pass it on to his son. He owned a house in Park Lane, some farms in various parts of the Home Counties, and an estate in the rural heart of his constituency, Mansfield Park.

The happy couple went on to have four children – Tom, Edmund, Maria and Julia. But Lady Bertram became very idle after the birth of the youngest and refused to go any further from her house than the garden and grounds. There was nothing really wrong with her, but she preferred to spend most of each day in her boudoir, nicely dressed, watching daytime television, eating chocolates and reading celebrity magazines. She said that she was delicate; others said that she had agoraphobia. She was prepared to show herself and chat affably a few times a year, when her husband gave parties for his constituency workers, but she absolutely refused to go to London.

After a while Sir Thomas had to accept that his wife was never going to do anything for his career. He was a hard worker, and everyone respected him, but his entire parliamentary life passed on the back benches. He served on several sub-committees and took several fact-finding trips abroad. When his children were old enough to go to boarding school he sold the London house and moved into a small service flat near Westminster. But he was quite popular in his constituency, and spent as many weekends at home as he could.

Mansfield Park was a spacious and elegant Georgian house set in grounds which had been landscaped, two hundred and fifty years before, by Capability Brown. There was a lake, a little Norman church with adjoining parsonage, some splendid cedars and oak trees. There were twelve bedrooms, four bathrooms, two grand reception rooms and a conservatory where Sir Thomas kept his cacti; he loved his collection and had brought home rare specimens from all over the world. The children were all healthy and good-looking and he and his wife got on as well as could be expected. The only problem, which no one had ever been able to solve, was finding servants.

2

Lady Bertram's Sisters

Lady Bertram was the second of three sisters. Their parents (long dead now) had hoped that Sir Thomas would introduce the other two to some eligible men, but for some reason nothing came of this. Neither of them made a very successful marriage.

The eldest was a small, angry woman, extremely plain and hyperactive. Her name was Desiree, but this was so unsuitable that it was hardly ever used. She had taught mathematics at a private school, but so terrified the children that she was asked to leave. Then she moved in with her sister and took over the housekeeping. At around this time the Reverend Stephen Norris, Mansfield's vicar, was causing concern. He was an elderly man who had recently lost his wife and become very vague and frail. Desiree marched into the vicarage, made his meals, did his laundry, got him through the Sunday services and eventually married him. She would run the parish council with an iron hand and keep her husband just alive for another six years.

When he died, Mrs. Norris moved into the former lodge at the iron gates of Mansfield Park. She paid no rent, and did not seem particularly upset. She continued to lay down the law to her sister's family, the Women's Institute and anybody else who was prepared to put up with her. As Sir Thomas was away for much of the time, and Lady Bertram did nothing, it was she who gave the gardener his orders and interviewed a string of foreign girls, few of whom lasted many months. The children called her 'aunt', or, behind her back, plain 'Norris'.

The third sister, Frances, married a man called Price, a lieutenant in the Navy, and had two children, but he disappeared when his ship was in the West Indies and was never seen again. Mrs. Norris said some scornful things and there was a bad quarrel. The sisters had no contact for several years.

3

Franny Price

'Frances has had *another* child'.

It was eleven in the morning. Lady Bertram, in her cream negligee sprinkled with yellow chrysanthemums, was sipping coffee and glancing through the *Daily Mail*. She looked up reluctantly at her sister, who had been dressed for hours.

'How many has she got now?'

'It's her fifth'.

'I keep forgetting'.

'You would', Mrs. Norris said contemptuously. 'She had two children, William and Franny, by her useless husband. I don't think they were ever divorced. Then she moved in with another man – she called him her partner – and had two more children, Susie and a boy. And now – '

'I thought a partner was somebody you danced with'.

'No, it means a relationship outside marriage. I warned her that the man wouldn't stay around and he didn't. And now she tells me that she's had another baby by yet another man. A third boy'.

'And is this man still –?'

'Of course not. She's on her own again, with all those children, and of course she wants the taxpayer, that means you and me, to support them. I knew how it was going to be when I went to Plymouth last year. So far as Frances herself is concerned, I have no hope. The eldest girl – Franny – is a stupid little thing, but she's already doing various jobs around the house which her mother is too lazy to do. She could be trained. The thing is – are you *listening*, Maria?'

Lady Bertram's eyelids jerked open.

'I lie awake at night worrying about that child. She's only ten. She'll go the same way as her mother in a few years, unless somebody does something. You may think it's no business of mine, but I happen to believe that one should assist one's neighbours and especially one's family. The boys are just healthy young animals, but it's not a good environment for a girl'.

'Yes. I mean, no'.

'So it occurs to me that it would be a kind action to bring her to Mansfield. If Thomas agrees, of course, but I'm certain he will. There's plenty of room, and she could make herself useful. It's a long time since we had a really satisfactory home help. Philomena is *most* idle –'

'Yes', Lady Bertram agreed. 'Forever on the phone to her boyfriend'.

' – and she's young enough to fit in. Everybody would benefit. We'll talk about it seriously when Thomas comes home this weekend'.

Sir Thomas made no difficulty. He found Mrs. Norris a trying woman, but he did not have to see much of her, and he was well aware that, without her, his home life would disintegrate. So it made sense to agree to whatever she wanted within reason, and he was sorry for the little girl.

'Just do what you think best, Desiree. She'll be company for you in your little gatehouse'.

But Mrs. Norris had no intention of having Franny under her own roof. There were three unoccupied rooms on the top floor of Mansfield Park.

4

Franny and her Cousins

Franny was nine, small, scrawny, fair-haired and extremely timid. She was overawed when Mrs. Norris swept into her mother's house, only the second time they had met, and picked her up. She had never been out of Plymouth in her life, and gazed out of the train window, wide-eyed, as they sped through Devon and Berkshire, clutching her battered and not very clean blue teddy bear. London and the crowded tube absolutely terrified her, as did Mrs. Norris herself. She kept hearing how grateful she should be for all that was being done for her, and kept repeating 'thank you very much'.

Sir Thomas's Bentley met them at the tiny Mansfield station, which stood just opposite the park gates. His great-grandfather had had it built on his land in the nineteenth century, enabling him to run up to London and back in one day. The rest of Mansfield village consisted of the church, the parsonage, some ancient almshouses and a new estate with an infant school and one general store.

The iron gates swung open at the touch of a fob, and Franny saw two great cedars, a glimpse of a bluebell wood, an avenue of rhododendrons in full bloom and one end of a lake. A grey-haired man who was trimming the borders waved to them. Then the house itself appeared, a splendid white house with pillars, and a pergola clothed in wisteria. She was speechless.

The chauffeur let them out. They entered a white marble hall, dominated by a large picture of water and buildings, a Canaletto which an earlier Bertram had picked up cheaply two hundred years ago. Up a grand staircase, and into a pleasant south-facing room where Lady Bertram and her television spent most of each day. Her aunt didn't get up, but greeted them with a friendly smile, and informed them that Philomena had just walked out.

'That girl was never any good', Mrs. Norris said briskly. 'We'll get a Romanian next time'. (This was before Brexit). 'Well, Franny, this is your chance to make yourself useful. Did anyone pack the dishwasher while I was away? No, I thought not. Franny, this is the small kitchen, and first thing, you can make us some tea'.

'Thank you very much', Franny blurted out.

She made tea, she was used to doing that. She gathered up the dirty mugs and glasses and washed them. Then Mrs. Norris marched her up some more stairs to her new room, an attic with a bed, chair, clothes rail and sink. There were two other tiny rooms and a lavatory in the corridor. She didn't mind, because there was a view of one end of the lake, and she had never before had a room to herself. She was told that she might share Maria and Julia's bathroom, on the floor below – 'so long as you never keep them waiting'. She soon learned to use a dishwasher and to do all sorts of other jobs. There was normally a girl from Bulgaria or the Philippines in residence, and an elderly lady, Mrs. Smith, who lived in Mansfield village, came in to do the heavy cleaning twice a week.

Sir Thomas appeared, and told her that he hoped she would be a good girl and help her aunts. She found him terrifying. Her cousins were all away, Tom and Eddy at Eton, and the girls at a boarding school in Sussex. She was not going to join them; she was to go to the junior school in Thorpe Milton, the town two stations down the line.

She first met her four cousins when they came home for the summer holidays. They were all tall, fair and good-looking. Tom, the eldest, was out with his friends most of the time and took little notice of her. Eddy was quieter, but she noticed that he passed her the marmalade without being asked and had a nice smile. Julia and Maria were two and three years older and she had a sinking feeling, almost straight away, that they despised her.

'She's stupid', Maria confided to their aunt on the first evening. 'Her clothes come from Oxfam'.

Mrs. Norris had always made a great fuss of her nieces and thought they were devoted to her.

'And she's got an awful west-country accent', said Julia, 'and she thinks a ball is something you kick about'.

'Now, girls', Mrs. Norris said, 'not everyone is as pretty and clever as you, but I know you'll be kind to the poor little thing, and she'll be grateful if you give her your old clothes. She doesn't come from a good home; we must make every allowance'.

Franny spent any free time she had wandering around and trying to take it all in. Once she got as far as the gates and peered through them at the tiny village which clung to the fringes of the Mansfield estate. These gates were usually locked, but the Parsonage had a back garden, separated from the park by a low wall. Most of the time, though, she never got outside the house. She was amazed to find that it had two staircases, one much more splendid than the other. There was a ballroom with a wonderful glittering chandelier; there were several paintings of long-dead Bertrams, the gentlemen in wigs and the ladies in beautiful dresses. It was overwhelming.

One day Eddy found her crying on the back stairs.

'Franny, what's the matter?' He sat down next to her. 'Has anyone been unkind to you?'

She clutched her blue bear, and shook her head.

'Tell me about it'.

In the end she told him that she missed her family, and particularly William, the brother closest to her in age.

'How many brothers and sisters have you got?'

'There are five of us including me. Susie, Sam and baby Charles, but William's the one I like best'.

'Well, we're your family too', Eddy said cheerfully. 'Your mother finds it difficult to look after five children by herself, so it's really better if you spend a few years living with us. I'll tell you what, let's turn on Skype, and talk to William. I'd like to meet him'.

'What's Skype?'

'Oh – it's a way of looking at people on your computer, having a long-distance conversation'.

'We haven't got a computer'.

'Okay'. Eddy pulled out his phone. 'We'll ring him up'.

He did, they caught William at home and all three of them got on very well.

That was when her adoration of Eddy began.

5

Franny and her Cousins (continued)

E ight years went by.
Franny changed from the lower to the upper school in
Thorpe Milton. The best part of her day was the long walk
across the park on her way to and from the station; Mr.
Hawkins the gardener often walked beside her to chat and
they became good friends. She dreaded the train journeys;
the rougher boys ganged up on her, laughed at her Devon
accent and blew cigarette smoke in her face. The children
had found out that she didn't live with her family and called
her 'carer girl'. Back at home, Mrs. Norris usually had
several jobs for her. On a good day, she could sneak upstairs
and make a start on her homework, but there was never
quite enough time, and she fell further and further behind.

In all those years she never visited her birth family.
William came for a fortnight, invited by Eddy, when he had
turned sixteen and just left school. He was unsure what he
wanted to do next, except to go round the world. When the
Plymouth family got a PC they sometimes talked on Skype,
but her mother was never the first to get in touch with her
and seemed hardly interested.

When she was fourteen she developed acne, a sad
contrast to Maria and Julia, who had flawless complexions.

When she was sixteen it was decided that she should leave school.

'She's not intelligent', Mrs. Norris said, 'and really, Thomas can't be expected to put her through university. She can be much more useful around the house'.

Franny herself was relieved. She had only two GCSEs, and ever since the acne flared up she had hated meeting people. Mrs. Norris (who slept in her own house, but visited Mansfield Park most days and ate all her meals there) could not be everywhere at once, and Lady Bertram was not at all frightening. She cooked, ran errands, answered the phone, did everything that was asked or expected. When Mr. Hawkins complained that the gardening was getting too much for him and he wanted a young assistant, she was ordered to help him. He told her the names and qualities of the various plants; Mrs. Norris never knew how much she loved this work. The grounds were thrown open three or four times a year for garden parties or charity events and Sir Thomas liked to see them looking good. It was soon agreed that, even if their niece had been fit for higher education, they could not have done without her.

None of the Bertram children wanted to go into politics. Tom was a worry. He had crashed his father's second car; he had failed his degree, he spent most of his time in London with unsuitable friends. Eddy had decided to be a teacher and was in his final year at training college. Franny lived for the times he came home, which were less often than she would have liked. When he discovered that she was afraid of dogs, he took her for long walks around the park with the two Afghan hounds until she got used to them. They watched the squirrels running up and down the great beech trunks and chatted about anything that came into his head.

'The rich man in his castle, the poor man at his gate', Eddy said, soon after she had got to know him. 'That's from a hymn we sang at school and it always made me think about the iron gates here at Mansfield. It doesn't seem fair, does it?'

'No', Franny echoed.

'Well, I'm never going to own this house and park. But I certainly have had a privileged upbringing and I think it's important to give something back. I'll tell Dad what I plan to do as soon as I'm sure'.

She adopted his beliefs quite naturally. These walks were the high point of her life, and he also took her out with his binoculars after dark and taught her the names of the stars. You had a good view of the night sky from the middle of the park.

The Bertram girls were not yet sure what they wanted to do.

'I do think' said Julia, 'that it was really mean of Dad to sell the London house. Everything's happening somewhere else and we just have to *stagnate* in the summer because nobody, who's anybody, wants to visit'.

'You're always running up to London', Eddy said mildly.

'I know, but he ought to have given Maria and me our own flat'.

Both girls had gone to Essex University. Julia, who was studying English, still had a year to do; Maria had taken an indifferent degree in journalism, and was drifting. She was very popular and had been photographed with several eligible young men. Julia, who was not quite so pretty or confident, had not yet had a serious boyfriend.

And then Maria announced her engagement. James Rushworth, usually known as Rush, was a heavyweight boxer who had become famous in the last two years. He was so huge and powerfully built that very few people could stand up against him. Suddenly pictures of Maria were splashed all over the papers and there were plans for a grand wedding in Mansfield church.

The year that Franny turned eighteen.

6

Mrs. Grant

The Mansfield drive was bordered with rhododendrons, pink and white and deep purple, looking their best on this particular Wednesday in May. Franny, with her trug and clippers, was hard at work when a car appeared and a cheerful-looking middle-aged lady wound down the window.

'Hello, aren't you one of the Bertram daughters?'

'No, I'm afraid not; I'm one of their cousins, Franny'.

'My name's Gillian Grant. Theo, my husband, is the new vicar, so you'll soon meet him, but he's hard at work just now writing about the Arian heresy. Jump in and show me the way'.

'I'm supposed –'

'Come on', Mrs. Grant said, throwing open the car door. 'I want to introduce myself to your family – Lady Bertram's an invalid, I understand, and her sister, Mrs. Norris, is the widow of a former vicar. I need a cup of coffee and I expect so do you. How far to the big house?'

Franny was used to doing what she was told. She said meekly, 'Half a mile', and climbed in.

Lady Bertram was with her hairdresser and could not be seen, but Mrs. Norris received them graciously in the

Yellow Room and told Franny to find Gabriela, the new Romanian maid, and bring coffee for their guest. She explained that Sir Thomas was away, and so were all the young Bertrams, but she certainly hoped that the two households would make friends.

'Theo's a recluse', laughed Mrs. Grant. 'He's interested in nothing but the history of the early church. Sadly we haven't any children. But I do have two young people coming to stay with us very soon, and I hope they'll get on with your own brood'.

Franny came in with a tray of coffee and Danish pastries.

'Henry and Missy – her real name is Mary – are my half-brother and half-sister. It's a complicated story. My mother got married when I was twelve, to a man called Ross Crawford, a banker, and had these two children. Then she died, and he got married again, to a younger woman I never really liked, to be honest. Then, a year ago, *he* died, and very soon afterwards this woman moved her boyfriend into the family home. Henry is a barrister and has a flat in Chelsea –'

Mrs. Norris registered these facts.

' – and is hoping to go into politics, and Missy wants to act. But unfortunately she never got on with her stepmother; last week there was a great row and she was forced to move out. She's a lovely girl and plays the harp beautifully. There's no room for her in Henry's little flat so he's going to drive her down tomorrow and stay for a bit. Now the seat next to Sir Thomas's, West Northamptonshire –'

'Franny', snapped Mrs. Norris, 'can't you find anything to do with yourself?'

As she slipped out, Franny noticed that Mrs. Grant seemed surprised, even a little shocked, but in fact she was relieved to get back to her gardening. Over supper with her aunts, she heard more about their new neighbours. The Crawfords were delightful young people, 'and very well off', Mrs. Norris said. Mrs. Grant herself was not well off; the money had come from their father, not their mother. Her job before she met the Doctor had been with a very respectable dating agency. 'They don't call them marriage bureaux now'.

7

The Crawfords

Miss Mary Crawford gazed at the crimson sunset behind the two cedars, as her brother Henry mixed them cocktails and an enticing smell of Beef Wellington drifted upstairs. Mrs. Grant was an excellent cook, and her husband, though he usually took little notice of his surroundings, very much enjoyed his food.

'You've got the most marvellous view of the park, Gill. I just saw two good-looking young men walking their dogs, are they the Bertram brothers?'

She had been thinking it was high time that she made a fresh start and met some decent men. Everything had gone wrong in her life since her beloved father got married again, and it had been much, much worse since he died. He had doted on her, paid for her to go to RADA, left her two million pounds, but she couldn't get hold of it until she was twenty-five, and that was eighteen months away. He had been afraid, of course, that she would marry the wrong man, and she could see, now it was too late, that she had been unwise to get mixed up with Andrew Stornoway. Her stepmother thought of him as her fiancé. She had been furious when she found out what was going on and Missy could never again live in the lovely Thameside house where she had grown up. She'd told her half-sister a version of the truth, and Gill had been kind and helpful, but she was not happy to have been dumped here in the middle of Northamptonshire. She thought, at least I can run up to London from the little station. I'll have to meet people, if I'm ever going to be a serious actor. I'll have to get an Equity card.

'Yes', said Gillian, 'they've just come home. Tom and his brother; he's going to be the next Sir Thomas Bertram'.

'How's that?'

'It's the hereditary principle', Henry explained. 'The current Sir Thomas has never done anything, so far as I'm aware, except sit on the back benches for about a century, but he's a baronet and his elder son inherits the title when he pops off. He'll probably also inherit the park and the rest of the land. That's how the British aristocracy have operated over hundreds of years. The younger sons get nothing'.

They're both attractive, Missy thought, but perhaps I'll like the elder son best.

'And there are two lovely girls', Mrs. Grant said, 'whom I haven't met –'

'So how do you know that they're lovely?' inquired Henry. 'Gill, I suspect that you're still encouraging people to marry each other. I'm only twenty-eight. I'm in no hurry'.

'Well, Henry, I've seen their photographs and they certainly look very pretty. I'm sure you'll want to get married one day, and if –'

'I know. I know you were about to say that if I'm going to be an MP I'll need a wife or a steady girlfriend. There are some local parties where I intend to show myself. Perhaps I could ask one of the Bertram girls –'.

'Julia', Mrs. Grant said promptly. 'Maria is engaged to that boxer, the one they call Rush'.

'He's gross', Missy said.

'Yes, he is, but we don't see very much of him. Mrs. Norris decides what goes on in that house, and she wants you all to meet'.

8

The Crawfords and the Bertrams

Mrs. Grant had worked for fifteen years with Marian Reed Introductions, which had brought about several very successful marriages, and although she was now a full-time clergy wife she couldn't get out of the mental habit of pairing people off. She was worried about her young half-sister.

Henry would be all right. He had his Chelsea flat, half of a cottage in Norfolk, two directorships, and a very good chance of becoming the candidate for West Northamptonshire, the seat adjoining Mansfield Park. Sir Thomas himself had an unshakeable majority, but his colleague had announced that he was standing down at the next election, and he had only just hung on last time. But Henry would make a good impression; he always did. If elected he wouldn't stagnate on the back benches like Sir Thomas but would climb very quickly. And when he wanted, he would naturally have no trouble finding a wife.

But Missy didn't have a proper income yet, or a career. She was a good mimic, she had a lovely singing voice, she played the harp to a high standard, but Gillian knew enough about the acting profession to realise how unlikely it was that she would get to the top. And now she had lost her home and it wasn't obvious what she could do next. If only she hadn't been so young when our mother died, she thought; if only her father hadn't married that woman. She herself had been alone for years before she met the much older Dr Grant, and she didn't want that for her sister. It would be such a good thing if Missy could meet a good man.

Once all four young Bertrams were at home, which happened soon afterwards, they and the Crawfords spent a delightful three weeks together. They went to London, to the Derngate theatre in Henry's car, they swam and boated in the lake, they turned up late at one or other house and expected Franny or Mrs. Grant to put a meal in front of them. Lady Bertram and Mrs. Norris looked on tolerantly and were glad that they were having fun. Sir Thomas hardly saw them.

Maria and Julia were both very struck with Henry. He was not very tall, and as dark as a Spaniard, but he was extremely charming and amusing. And it was quite likely that he would become a colleague of their father's. What Sir Thomas knew of him, he approved.

Missy thought, at first, that she preferred Tom Bertram. Both brothers were handsome and pleasant, but once she had had a good look at the house and park she reminded herself that the elder would eventually own them. But after a week Tom took himself off; he said he couldn't stand the country without a car and had no idea when he'd be back. It was obvious that he was not interested.

'He smashed Dad's car', Julia confided to her new friend.

'Oh, dear. Was he drunk?'

'Yes, actually he's lucky to be alive. Dad was really fed up. He keeps saying that he'll have to sell the Canaletto if Tom goes on like this and doesn't know why he can't settle down and get a job like he did at that age'.

Julia had also been confiding in Eddy. 'Missy's told me all about her stepmother, a hateful woman. She moved her boyfriend in as soon as her husband died, and made it impossible for her to stay in her own home'.

Eddy was sorry to hear this. He liked Missy, but he thought that certain things shouldn't be talked about outside the family; he himself would never have told a new acquaintance that he didn't agree with his father politically or that his mother was extremely idle. Still, there was no doubt that the poor girl had had a bad time.

And she was such a good musician. She played the harp for them, one evening when bats were hovering around the Parsonage garden, and all were very impressed. Eddy stood close behind her. She played Mozart first, and then another haunting tune that Franny couldn't recognise. She was so beautiful and sophisticated – lustrous dark hair, a great deal of it, sparkling dark eyes, a delightful caressing voice. Afterwards they urged her to sing to them.

Franny went out of the gate, unnoticed, sat down on the dry grass under the cedar and looked up at the darkening summer sky. She remembered how Eddy, long ago, had taught her to identify the stars.

James Rushworth, who had been touring the States, had not been seen recently. When he came back, he invited them to visit his country home, Sotherton, where he and Maria were going to live part time, and his mother was living already. It was thirty miles from Mansfield, and there was some discussion about travel plans.

'I think everyone can fit into Henry's Jaguar', Mrs. Grant said, as she was drinking tea with the older members of the family. 'There's you, Desiree, Henry, Eddy, Maria and Julia, and you, Franny. Thank you –' this to Franny who was handing round slices of lemon cake. She understood by now that Lady Bertram did not go anywhere.

'That's very kind', Mrs. Norris said rather sharply, 'but Franny can't be spared. My sister isn't strong and has to have somebody with her'.

'That's so', Lady Bertram said placidly.

This was very strange, Gillian thought. The woman looked perfectly healthy, and didn't they have the Romanian maid, Gabriela? And the poor girl was blushing to hear herself talked about. Impulsively she said, 'Don't worry about that, Lady Bertram. I'd love to spend the day with you, if you allow me. I have some videos which I'm sure would interest you'.

'How kind', said Lady Bertram, and Mrs. Norris looked enraged.

'Now, Franny', Mrs. Norris said, as Henry smilingly opened the doors of his dark red Jaguar, 'this is a great treat for you, and I hope you're grateful to your cousins and Mrs. Grant. And make sure you thank Mrs. Rushworth; I can't trust you to speak pleasantly when I'm not with you. Do you understand?'

'Yes, aunt', Franny said meekly, as she did a dozen times a day.

Henry was arranging them; Julia was invited to take the front seat; Maria, Franny and Mrs. Norris got into the back and Eddy squashed in the boot. Franny looked out at the green countryside whirling past, all the scenes that she normally never saw, and was quietly thrilled. They drove through little stony villages, crossed a wide river, saw fields scattered with poppies. Maria, on the other hand, although she had been looking forward to showing her family her future home, felt inexplicably depressed. Her sister was openly flirting with Henry, and he didn't seem to mind; she had thought until now that she was the one he preferred. And as the wedding drew closer, and it became more and more difficult to change her plans, she had begun to wonder whether she really liked Rush so very much. If she compared him with either of her brothers, or with the seriously attractive man sitting in front of her, he seemed almost – boring. His programme was so full and his training so intensive that she had hardly seen him for weeks. It doesn't mean anything, she told herself. It's just last-minute nerves.

They swept up the lime avenue (planted in March 1916 after a great gale) and into the courtyard of Sotherton. Franny immediately thought that she liked the grounds better than the house, which was Elizabethan, about a hundred years older than Mansfield Park, and heavy-looking. There was a wood not far away. Beeches, copper beeches, oaks and chestnuts; she would love to get away from the rest of the party and explore.

Mrs. Rushworth, a plump little woman, and her son were waiting for them on the terrace. They were given glasses of Pimms and escorted over the ground floor, very large dignified rooms with moulded ceilings and Victorian fireplaces. There was a dining-room with a vast mahogany table and some William Morris wallpaper which, Maria said, she was going to rip down. They would cut down the elderly limes, too, and have an open-air swimming pool. The tour ended in the family chapel, which had some memorial tablets to long-dead owners on the walls. This was to become a snooker room.

Everywhere they saw giant framed photographs of Rush, and posters about his famous fights. His mother, who had an estuary accent like his own, had attached herself to Missy and was proudly telling her, 'his teachers always said that he'd never do nothing, but you can just see how he's turned out'.

'Well, how wrong they were, Mrs. Rushworth', Missy said politely. 'Those who can, do, and those who can't, teach'.

There was a horrid silence.

'Oh, dear! Have I said something awful?'

'You have rather', said Julia. 'Eddy is going to be a teacher'.

Franny, trying to conceal herself behind Rush's vast shoulders, admired the way Missy instantly reacted.

'Eddy, I'm so sorry. Actually I know absolutely nothing about anything, but if I *had* known I wouldn't have said –'

'That's all right'.

'Do tell me'. She went up to him smiling; she was much shorter and smaller than he was. 'What exactly is your job?'

'Well, I'm starting in September. A comprehensive in North London. The children speak about ten different languages and it's trying to come out of special measures. I'm going to be thrown in at the deep end'.

'That sounds very tough indeed. I'm impressed'.

They were still talking earnestly as they strolled outside, and people drifted apart. Mrs. Norris was interrogating the Polish couple who waited on them; the wife cooked and the husband was an odd job man and occasional butler. The gardens looked neglected, as the house had not been lived in for two years. No doubt Maria had plans. They entered the fringe of the woods and Franny found herself walking along a winding path just behind Eddy and Missy, who seemed quite absorbed in one another.

Beneath the giant beeches, it was cool and pleasant. But her head was beginning to ache and she wished she could find some excuse to be left by herself. After a while they came to a small clearing where there was a dry fountain, with the statue of a boy holding a marble bowl, and an aged stone seat.

She thankfully sank down on it.

'Do go on', she said nervously. 'I'm a little tired'.

'Oh, dear, Franny', Missy said, 'are you too hot?'

'We'll stay with you', Eddy chimed in.

'No, please, don't bother'.

Missy sat beside her for a moment and then jumped up. 'You stay here, Eddy; I'll just go on a little way; I'd like to take some photos'.

'Don't get lost', said Eddy. 'Franny, will you be all right for five minutes?'

She assured him that she would. And they were gone.

About quarter of an hour went by. Then Rush appeared, breathing rather hard and sweating.

'Oh!' he exclaimed abruptly – he'd forgotten her name. 'Have you seen Maria?'

'I'm afraid I haven't, James'.

'Oh. She wanted me to get the summerhouse key. It's shut but we're going to smarten it up for parties. I was as quick as I could but when I came back, she was gone'.

'I'm so sorry. If I see her, shall I – ?'

'Blast!' He charged off into the trees.

Another ten minutes passed. Then Julia, also panting, came around a dead rhododendron bush.

'Have you seen Henry?'

'I haven't seen anyone, Julia. What have you been doing?'

'Mrs. Rushworth pinned me down. That woman's the worst bore in the entire universe. Did you hear her awful accent? I'm just thankful *I'm* not the one who's going to marry Rush. I need some air. Did you see him, Franny?'

'Henry? No, I haven't seen him since we came outside'.

'Well, you're the lucky one. Sitting in the shade relaxing. Never in my whole life have I endured such a boring woman. I'm off'.

She disappeared. After another interval, Eddy and Missy came back. Their heads were close together, and she thought for a moment that they were holding hands, but they were not. They were full of apologies for having left her so long.

It was time – high time, Eddy realised with a shock when he had checked – to return to the house. They found everyone sitting around the dining room table; Henry and Maria having strolled in a few minutes before. They seemed in high spirits, but Rush still looked annoyed. Mrs. Norris did most of the talking. The housekeeper brought them a very good supper; white wine, a cold venison pie, salad, a bowl of raspberries with cream and a crumbly French cheese. After coffee, served in tiny mint green Wedgwood cups, it was finally time to go.

Julia immediately brightened up when Henry again invited her into the front seat. They laughed and chatted all the way home, while behind them, Mrs. Norris talked interminably, Franny looked out of the window at the rising moon, and Maria sat back with a small, secret smile.

9

Tom's Party

Next morning, Franny got up at her usual time and took a last depressing look at her spots in her cracked bedroom mirror. She had just come down the first flight of stairs and got as far as Maria's door, which was half open, when she heard James Rushworth's tremendous voice, issuing from his phone '- that man Crawford'.

'I can't help it', Maria said coldly, 'if other men like me. Really, Rush –'.

'He's quite a little man. I could knock him down with one hand tied behind me. Why was your phone turned off all night?'

Oh dear!

She hurried past the voices and down the main staircase. Tom's expensive bag had been dropped in the hall; he must have just got off the early train. In the breakfast room, Gabriela, with a dark look, was spooning out scrambled eggs, and Julia, Tom and Eddy were deep in conversation.

'Hi', her cousin said, just glancing round as she came in. 'Fran, we're having a party on Friday, and can you –?'

'That isn't decided yet', said Eddy. 'Thank you, Gabriela. Franny, we were just discussing –'

'My birthday party. We've got four days, only just time to get organised. We'll have the Crawfords, of course, and I've already told about seventy people –'

'I thought you were going to celebrate your birthday in London'.

'I was, but this is a much better idea. John Yates had a cancellation – someone died – and he's bringing his band, they're going to perform for free. Dancing in the ballroom. Swimming in the lake. All those spare bedrooms. I've checked the forecast and it's perfect, a dry night and a full moon. Now, Franny, if you and Gabriela get moving –'

Gabriela stalked out. Eddy pushed back his chair and said, 'Tom, you know you can't do that'.

Franny knew exactly what he was talking about. Tom's twenty-first birthday party, four years ago, had been such a disaster that he had been forbidden ever again to hold one in the big house. She had been only fourteen then, and had gone to bed early, but she had heard the uproar and seen the broken windows and the pools of sick the next day. She felt cold and shocked.

'If you're thinking about the old man', Tom said, 'he won't know'.

Sir Thomas was in Singapore and not expected back for a week.

'You know he said no more of your parties at Mansfield'.

'Are you going to tell him?'

'No, but well, after all, it's his house'.

'It's my inheritance. You don't get it, Ed, this is your chance to hear the *John Yates Four*! In your own home! For free! You'll love it, won't you, Jules?' Julia nodded emphatically. 'We'll clear up long before Dad gets back.

Mum and Norris won't mind. In fact she'll probably organise it herself'. He rushed out and could be heard calling loudly for his aunt.

'This is awful', said Eddy.

'Don't be a killjoy, Ed', said Julia. 'The John Yates band is terrific'.

'Dad is sure to find out'. He got up, almost groaning. 'I'll have a word with Norris; she just might see sense'.

He knew, however, that there was nothing he could do stop it.

Neither his mother nor his aunt had the smallest objection. Lady Bertram was assured that she need do nothing, and Mrs. Norris threw herself eagerly into Tom's plans. There was soon a whirlwind of activity. She ordered vast quantities of food and drink, but decided not to order flowers; their own gardens could be stripped and that would save Sir Thomas expense. Hundreds of yellow balloons were arranged in the ballroom. Tom walked about from morning to night shouting into his phone; Franny kept hearing the phrase 'one of the great bands of our time'. She also heard Missy saying, 'of course we'll come, Tom; how lovely, and may I bring my harp?'

The Honourable John Yates and his friends turned up in their van on Friday afternoon. He was a tall weedy young man, very casually dressed, with mousy hair in a ponytail. There were two other men and a girl, and they took no notice of anyone except Julia and Tom.

All day the temperature had been soaring, and Franny had been kept busy cutting and arranging roses and ferns to decorate the public rooms. Hoping for five minutes to herself, she almost fell on to the nearest sofa, but a moment later Mrs. Norris ordered her to get up and attend to their guests.

'Gabriela's got a boyfriend', she said angrily. 'I've no idea where she picked him up. I just caught them on the phone, and I made it very clear that there won't be any goings-on in this house. You'd better keep a sharp eye on her, Franny. This is all getting too much for me; I really can't be expected to do everything myself'.

'Have you *heard* of the John Yates Four?' Missy asked her brother as she put the finishing touches to her eye make-up.

'I have just about. I think he was at Eton with Tom'.

'Well, Tom is behaving as if he'd just swallowed a wheelbarrow of amphetamines. Eddy isn't happy; he thinks his father wouldn't approve. Which I can well believe. I'm going to open the concert'.

She was wondering whether Tom had come home with the idea of seeing her; he had certainly seemed very keen to have her at his party. She might take another look at him.

'You are coming, aren't you?'

'It all sounds rather adolescent', said Henry. 'Yes, I'll drop in and applaud you, but, really, I've had almost enough of Mansfield'.

An hour later, the ballroom which had hosted so many graceful dances and refined soirees over the last two centuries was crowded with Tom's friends and acquaintances, and the concert began. Missy played a Bob Dylan tune, rather well, on her harp. There was some polite clapping, but then the John Yates Four almost elbowed her aside and were greeted with shrieks of rapture. They started to perform. A young woman in purple began to sing in a high wild voice. They could be heard all over Mansfield village and at the Parsonage half a mile away.

Mrs. Norris had a violent headache. Try as she would, she didn't think that she could stand much more, and she also felt that these young people were treating her, the organiser of the party, with very little respect. She gave Franny and Gabriela their orders and then poured herself a stiff drink, took three aspirins and made a final tour of the upper floors. To her horror, she found a young man and woman clamped together on a bed, and sternly told them that these rooms were private. They went off, giggling. Lady Bertram was serenely watching television and hardly noticed her. She stumped back to the gatehouse, undressed, and remained unconscious for the whole of the night.

The noise level mounted. People from Thorpe Milton and as far away as Northampton had heard about the party and turned up, uninvited. Miss Mary Crawford secured her harp and detached herself from the crowd; she was not used to being overlooked. Tom was leaping about the floor like a demented grasshopper; she couldn't think what she had ever seen in him. She looked around for Eddy, but he was being introduced to Gabriela's boyfriend and pouring him a drink. She thought how unfortunate it was that she was always tired out by ten o'clock; if she was ever going to be a professional actor she would need to get used to late nights. The heat was quite intolerable. She edged out, through the hall and porch, on to the terrace where she thankfully dropped down on the lowest step and gazed at the full moon. It was casting a broad stream of light on the lake and she thought she could see figures moving about on the bank. She decided that she couldn't face the walk home and must find Henry, and then, out of the dark, she heard someone say his name. Sir Thomas's daughters were standing just outside the house and arguing in low tense voices.

'I think that marriage ought to *mean* something!'

'I'm not married'.

'I think it's *sickening*!'

'Julia, I can't see why I shouldn't spend time with Henry; he's a very interesting man'.

'Which is more than anyone can say for Rush'.

'You're just jealous because you can't get a man yourself'.

'So I *can*!'

Missy thought, it's high time those girls grew up. She quietly walked back into the house and looked for her brother. She saw Franny carrying a tray of drinks, Gabriela and her boyfriend in the kitchen, eating canapés and kissing in the intervals of washing up, the girl in the skimpy purple dress staggering out alone into the dark. Then, to her relief, she spotted him coming out of the lavatory.

'Henry, please could you drive me and the harp home?'

'Had enough?' asked Henry, feeling for his keys. 'You always did flake out halfway through the evening. Let's go'.

He opened the car for her, saying that he wasn't going to drink, and a minute later put her down at the Parsonage door.

'Are you coming in?'

'No, I'll just go back and thank our host. What a dolt he is. Actually I could stay awake for hours, but it's the worst party I've seen for some time'.

Missy let herself in and went straight to bed. She didn't feel strong enough to talk to her sister, but could distinctly hear Dr Grant complaining that, with this fearful cacophony going on, he could neither work nor sleep.

Franny's head was swimming. She had been circulating for hours, passing drinks to people who accepted them without a word of thanks, and didn't know how much longer she could stay on her feet. She saw Henry Crawford dancing with Maria, saying something close to her ear, and then saw them leave the ballroom together. She saw Julia watching them, looking horrified.

She supported herself against the wall.

Sometime later, Eddy came up.

'Franny, you look terrible!' She thought she probably did. 'Please do go to bed; you've had enough for tonight. Gabriela and Pete are doing everything necessary, and I'm going to stay up for as long as it takes. We'll be fine'.

Somebody had obviously been inside her room. The bed was disarranged, the toothmug had been used and there were cigarette stubs in the sink and on the floor. She opened the window to let out the smell and heard more shouting. Fortunately, the door had an old-fashioned key, and she felt safer once she had locked herself in.

John Yates and his friend Brick sat smoking in the dimly lit conservatory. The other two members of the quartet were nowhere to be seen. They had had a long day, had drunk a good deal, and their thoughts were turning to bed, but it seemed too much effort to get up yet.

'That's – a lot of – different kind of – cactuses', Brick spluttered.

'Yeah, I thought they all – looked the same'.

'Little flowers on some of them and – little prickles –'

'Cool'.

'They've got – giant cactuses – in the Mexican desert –'

'Yeah'.

'I think if you – lit up – those little hairs – look spectacular –'

Brick heaved himself on to his feet. He brought out his lighter and lurched from pot to pot, illuminating each cactus on his way. John Yates laughed helplessly and again said, 'Cool'. But after a moment a fire alarm went off, the flames spread, and the two young men ran out of the conservatory calling loudly for help.

In the end, it was a fairly small tragedy. Eddy beat out the flames with his jacket while somebody rang 999; the outer doors were flung open and the fire brigade arrived from Thorpe Milton within minutes. Lady Bertram and some of the partygoers slept through everything. Franny heard the alarm and went halfway down the stairs in her dressing-gown, but was told that it was under control. The firefighters went away, assuring everyone that they and the house were safe. But Eddy could have wept as he looked at the blackened remains of Sir Thomas's cacti, the finest private collection in the Midlands, assembled in twenty-five years from all over the world, and kept repeating to Julia, who was also looking shocked, 'it's my fault'.

Franny woke up very early.

Everything was quiet now, and the cigarette smell had gone. She lay there for a while and wondered whether she had really seen Henry Crawford and Maria leave the party together, or whether she had been dreaming – there had been so many disturbances during the night. Yes, she decided, she certainly had seen them, and Julia had seen them too. She thought, guiltily, that she couldn't leave Gabriela to clear up everything and that Mrs. Norris would be furious if she found her still in bed. She got up, and stared unhappily at her face in the tiny mirror; her spots had flared up overnight and she looked awful, as Eddy had said.

She didn't dare to use her cousins' bathroom in case she bumped into Henry Crawford, so she washed at the sink and got dressed. Then she opened the curtains and glanced out at the lake as she did first thing every morning.

The body of a young woman was floating in the water, upside down.

10

How do you solve a problem like Maria?

Missy had fallen asleep as soon as her head hit the pillow. At first light she began to wake up, and listened for a while to the cooing of wood pigeons in Mansfield Park. Then there was a gentle knock on her door and Henry, fully dressed, came in.

'Did I wake you?'

'Not at all'. Missy sat up briskly. 'Let's go down and have breakfast'.

'I'm leaving, I'm afraid. Can you make my excuses to Gill? I need to get to London before anyone catches me'.

Missy looked automatically at her little watch; it was quarter to five.

'Henry, what *is* going on?'

'I'm afraid I have a problem with Maria'.

A moment's silence.

'You went back to the party – wasn't it awful? – and –'

'I didn't mean to stay, but I bumped into her –'

'Henry, did you –?'

'Well, yes, but now I rather wish I hadn't. She was very clinging, almost hysterical, kept saying that she was in love with me –'

'You do know, Henry, that the woman's about to get married?'

'Doesn't everyone know? I think that's a matter for her and not me. Oh, and an alarm went off at midnight, I thought I was going to be caught red-handed, but Maria checked and said that it wasn't serious. Some idiot playing with matches. Anyway, I have a great deal to do in London, and I intend to lie low for a while. I hope you won't be bored, Missy. I'll come back and collect you and the harp whenever you like, but I've really got to go'.

'Well, presumably the marriage is off', said Missy. 'Poor Maria, and poor Rush. Henry, you've been up all night, are you sure you're fit to drive?'

'Oh, I'll be fine. The roads are almost empty, and it's a lovely day'.

Missy tried to go back to sleep, but couldn't. In the end she got up, had a shower and put on a vivid gold and green summer dress. She went downstairs and began to make coffee but, just before the kettle boiled, she happened to glance out of the window and saw Maria Bertram in the park with the two Afghan hounds, staring at the empty place where Henry's Jaguar should have been. She looked terrible.

Impossible to pretend that she hadn't seen her. She unlocked the door and called out, 'Hello, Maria, do come in'.

Maria entered slowly.

'I was – taking the dogs for a walk'.

So Henry had sneaked out while she was asleep. It was too bad of him. She said brightly, 'Have a chair; I'm making some real coffee. I went home early last night. I'm a lark, not an owl, and it was getting too noisy'.

Mrs. Grant, wide awake and in a threadbare pink dressing-gown, walked in.

'Oh, hello, Maria, dear, lovely to see you. Coffee, that's just what I need. Did you enjoy the party?'

'I'm afraid the music got on Theo's nerves', Missy said.

'Oh, you know what he's like. Even when he was a student he hated parties. Missy, have you any idea what's happened to Henry? I'm sure I heard his voice, but his car isn't here'.

Now for it. Missy turned her back on them both while she brewed some very strong Italian coffee, and said the lines she had prepared.

'Henry asked me to apologise. He stayed on for a few hours because of the party, but he always meant to go home today. Half his things are in London, and he has to see a great many people. He knew you wouldn't mind'.

'He's made a lot of friends and contacts here', said Mrs. Grant. 'I do hope they like him. Wouldn't it be nice, Maria, if he and your father were in Parliament at the same time? But, really, it's rather naughty of him to take off and not say goodbye'.

Missy opened a carton of double cream.

'It's typical, I'm afraid'.

'And of course the next big event is your wedding, Maria. We're very excited. Who are you going to have for bridesmaids? – Julia, of course, and Franny?'

Maria seemed stunned. She said with an obvious effort, 'Julia but not Franny – an old school friend –'

Gillian Grant thought, She doesn't sound at all enthusiastic; I wonder if she's having second thoughts. It's not too late to change her mind. She looked around for another subject. 'So now it's the morning after, and you'll have a lot of clearing up to do'.

'Yes', Maria said slowly. 'Something was going on near the lake'.

11

Tom's Party: the Aftermath

Franny rushed down the main staircase, into a hall full of exploded balloons. There was still a smell of burning. Eddy was standing near the door talking quietly to Gabriela's Pete and another man. She gasped out what she had seen, and they all ran outside.

Two of them plunged into the lake, which was waist-deep at that point, and brought out the dripping body of the young girl. Eddy began to apply artificial resuscitation, but it was obvious to everyone else that nothing could be done. Franny recognised the purple dress and long dank hair of the lead singer. She dropped on to her knees on the dewy grass and cried.

For the second time since midnight, there were frantic phone calls. An ambulance drove up, followed by a police car, and as they examined the corpse and asked questions John Yates, half dressed, stumbled out into the fresh air. He looked stunned and kept muttering, 'Little Sylvie, that's dire!' Another young man was telling a policewoman, 'I didn't see her after the concert. Somebody said something about going for a splash'.

And while all this was happening a taxi drove up to the main entrance, and Sir Thomas Bertram got out.

The awful morning passed. After the paramedics had confirmed that life was extinct, covered the body and driven it away, they went into the house and the police officers took statements from John Yates and his two colleagues, from Eddy, and from Sir Thomas, who told them that he had caught an earlier than expected flight from Singapore and had no idea what had been going on. Tom was woken up and brought downstairs, complaining bitterly about his head. Franny made coffee for everyone; the remaining guests, after their names and statements had been taken down, went away. Only Lady Bertram, having said two or three times that it was very sad, sailed calmly through it all.

Sylvie had been a key member of the John Yates Four, they said, and had a lovely voice. She had been saying she was overheated, and had been seen to go out. Yes, there had been some talk about moonlight swimming. Yes, she might have taken some pills, people did all the time. Where did her parents live? Well, she had a mother, who was thought to be in France.

Nobody knew who told the press, but they found out long before midday.

When the police had done their work and left, Sir Thomas was finally able to confront his family. He was jet-lagged, had intended to go straight to bed, and was more upset by the destruction of his cactus collection than by the death of a girl he did not know, but what especially angered him was the way his children had staged the party behind his back. If his wife had been like other people, he reflected, the family could have got on perfectly well without Mrs. Norris.

'Desiree, I am surprised', he said. 'Surprised and disappointed. You must have been aware that, had I known, I would never have given my permission for this – this *rave*'.

Mrs. Norris was ashamed to admit that she had never thought about him. She said that she had only wanted the young people to have a good time, and that it was all the fault of John Yates.

'I know the family. They are not the sort of friends I want for my children. Kindly keep them away from this house in future'. Mrs. Norris indicated that they had already left. 'And now, I suppose, I must speak to my sons'.

Both young men were summoned to his study.

'I am ashamed of you, Tom. I had hoped that one day you would follow me into Parliament, but you are obviously quite unfit for public life. You knew my wishes perfectly well and you chose to flout them. You are not a teenager but a man of twenty-five. I just wish that you could model yourself on a young man like Henry Crawford, who is only a little older than you but already preparing to serve his country. And as for John Yates –'

'I only asked him', Tom said sulkily, 'because Julia likes his band'.

'Please don't drag your sister into this. Now, the press are aware of this disgraceful business, and I absolutely *forbid* you to talk to them. A taxi will call in half an hour to take you to Thorpe station; I don't care where you go after that. I don't want to see you again for some time. You may leave'.

Tom backed out and Sir Thomas turned to his younger son.

'I blame you too, Edmund. If you or the girls had picked up a phone and told me about it, none of this would have happened'.

'Dad, I really am sorry', Eddy blurted out. 'I'd just like to say, none of it was Franny's fault'.

'I never supposed that it was. Now, here is my statement for the Press Association. Take it down. "My wife and I are grieved and shocked by the death of" – what was the girl's name?'

'Sylvie Stratton-Booth'.

'Yes. "Our thoughts and prayers are with her family. We do not yet know how such a tragedy could have happened, but are working closely with the police and hope to find some answers". Get it done, and make it clear that I was out of the country and knew absolutely nothing'.

'Okay'.

As Eddy left the room, he passed Franny and Gabriela cleaning up the mess, and heard his sisters, upstairs, having a terrible scene.

By this time, Missy knew what had happened. She texted Eddy, saying that she was deeply sorry and sympathetic, but thought it best to stay where she was. Dr Grant had walked across the park to offer his condolences. Missy watched, with an interested eye, as various cars drove, or tried to drive, through the iron gates. She saw John Yates and his two surviving friends go away in their van. She also saw some men try and fail to get admitted and saw one of them hoist himself over the wall. She kept checking the news. Photographs of the house, and the lake, and the drowned girl, and of Sir Thomas and of the John Yates Four, were already circulating. People on Twitter were saying that this behaviour was typical of upper-class yobs and that Sir Thomas should probably be charged with manslaughter.

Around two in the afternoon, Eddy turned up at the Parsonage. He looked haggard, distraught, and it seemed quite natural to fall into his arms.

'I'm so sorry that you've been dragged into this'.

'That's all right, Eddy', Missy said, 'don't worry about me. What a terrible tragedy!'

'I've just been talking to her mother, the worst thing I've ever had to do. She's rushing back from France; she blames our family –'

'Eddy, that's ridiculous'.

'But, don't you see, it's partly my fault. None of this would have happened if I'd informed Dad, only it seemed mean. He's furious. The cactus collection meant a lot to him; he says he's going to prosecute John Yates. I did honestly try to keep everything under control. But the cacti don't really matter. I just can't stop thinking, I was talking to that poor girl only twelve hours ago, and now she's *dead*, and I keep thinking I could have stopped it –'

He was openly sobbing. Missy stroked his hair and he said, just audibly, 'I love you, I'll love you forever'.

12

Maria's Wedding

Franny was watering the geraniums in the great urns on the patio. It was a hot afternoon, four days after the dreadful party, and it was soothing to look at the white butterflies hovering round the lavender borders which she had just trimmed, and to be by herself. She could hear the adults' voices through the open French window, but hardly listened. She had been at work for half an hour when a shadow fell across the sun-splashed pavement, and there was Missy.

'Hello, Franny, hard at work?' She dropped down gracefully on to the warm stone. 'I love this weather. How are you?'

She was in a perfect cornflower-blue dress, with bare brown arms and legs and expensive sandals. Beautiful and sophisticated, while she, Franny, was wearing her ancient gardening clothes, and her spots, which she had checked an hour ago, looked even worse than usual.

'I've got something important to tell you'.

Franny could unfortunately guess what it was.

'Yes?'

'Eddy and I are an item'.

'Oh'.

'I've never felt anything like this before', Missy said dreamily. 'I've had other relationships, of course, but never with anyone I actually considered marrying. Isn't he wonderful, Franny? You must have known him all your life'.

'About half of it'.

'You're so lucky. It's hard to imagine Eddy as a little boy; he's so mature and sensible. The only problem – Well, this is our plan; Eddy's already got a room in a shared house near Seven Sisters Road, and now someone is moving out so I'll move in. We're going up to look at it today. We'll have to live like students, sharing the kitchen and bathroom with three other people – I hope it's clean! – not that I'll mind anything if I'm with him. Franny, why do you think that Eddy wants to *teach*?'

Franny tried to control the burning tears; she rubbed her eyes, hoping Missy would think it was because of the bright sunlight. Of course she had always known that something like this was bound to happen; nobody could help falling in love with Eddy. She said, 'He's always wanted that'.

'But it seems so unnecessary. It isn't even a good school, just a bog-standard comprehensive, and the pay is hardly enough to live on'.

Most unusually, Franny flared up.

'Eddy isn't doing it for the pay. He believes that it's not right for some children to get an expensive education – like he did, and my cousins, while everyone else goes to – what you call bog-standard –'.

She trailed off, horrified that she had said so much.

Missy smiled. 'But you didn't, did you, Franny?'

'I went to Thorpe Milton Upper School. I'm not clever'.

'I'm sure you are. Eddy says that his parents didn't bother with your education'.

'Oh. I didn't mind'.

'Well, I admire his principles, but I'm certain he can't do this for ever. From what he tells me, teachers burn out very quickly. His father could surely get him a proper job, or Henry could find something. He likes him; he's delighted that we're a couple. Oh, hi, Julia'.

Julia, who always looked depressed these days, had stepped out of the French window.

'Hi. Franny, could you go inside, please; Dad wants you'.

Sir Thomas and Lady Bertram, Mrs. Norris and Maria, were sitting in the shaded breakfast room drawing up wedding plans. Her uncle, who had been noticeably kinder to her in the last few days, was checking some figures and saying 'a new outfit'.

'Ah, Franny, there you are. Give me your number, my dear'.

'My number?'

'Your phone number'.

'I haven't got a phone, uncle'.

'Really? I thought everybody had. Well, you must get one immediately and – how old are you, Franny?'

'I was eighteen in –'

'A legal adult, then. Though I confess I thought you were much younger. We must put you on the voters' list. And since you *are* an adult, you must have a bank account and a reasonable allowance. I'll arrange –'

'Franny gets her board and lodging', Mrs. Norris snapped.

'Yes, Desiree, but every young person needs a little spending money. Please let me proceed. Now' – he turned to his wife – 'what's the name of that woman who comes to the house to choose your clothes?'

'Cynthia', Lady Bertram said with more animation than usual. 'She's marvellous'.

'Well, speak to her and make sure that Franny has a suitable dress for the wedding. Everything must be done well. I hope it may remove the unpleasant impression – '.

He fell silent, but everyone knew what he meant and what he wished. In private, Sir Thomas had a low opinion of his daughter's fiancé. It was impossible not to see that the young man was coarse and stupid, but Maria was a grown woman, and he was her choice.

No announcement appeared in the *Times* or the *Daily Telegraph* to say that the marriage of Miss Maria Bertram and Mr. James Rushworth would not take place. For three days Maria had agonised, hoping that Henry would at least send an apology or a bunch of flowers, but he did not. She had never felt so humiliated. Meanwhile the newspapers, which had reported the tragedy at Mansfield Park in great detail, were printing more and more inaccurate stories about Rush and herself. A glossy magazine featured a profile of her, calling her 'the girl who tamed him'. They had shown pictures of all his previous girlfriends and explained why she was 'different'. Preparations for 'the wedding of the year' were steaming ahead and would be very hard to stop.

Rush was away most of the time, training for his next big fight, so it wasn't easy to work out how she really felt about him. She had liked him well enough once, she was certain. And if she ended it, what sort of life could she expect? She didn't have a job, or a London base, or an income she thought she could live on. She hesitated for another week, which seemed a very long time, and asked no one's advice.

In the end, she decided that she couldn't bear Henry Crawford to think that she had given up this brilliant marriage because of him. Nobody else would know, but he would. And after all – she kept reminding herself – marriage was not a life sentence these days.

Julia was all in favour of it. The two sisters had had some bitter arguments but, once they were quite sure that Henry had gone, they made peace. Perhaps Julia had not quite given up hope herself, but in any case she wanted to see Maria safely married, and she also wanted to get away from Mansfield Park. There would always be a spare bedroom in the Rushworths' country home at Sotherton or in their London flat. Her bridesmaid's dress was very flattering.

The inquest on Sylvie Stratton-Booth recorded a verdict of death by misadventure. Her mother was very bitter, and said in court that it was Sir Thomas Bertram's fault, but everyone knew this was absurd as he hadn't been aware that the party was happening or even been in England at the time. The young woman had drunk a great deal and had taken some pep pills, and told a friend that she wanted to go swimming, although no one had seen her go into the lake. John Yates came up with a rambling story about a Chinese poet who had drowned trying to kiss the moon's reflection. He didn't seem upset.

Cynthia, a nice little woman in her forties who had done very well out of Lady Bertram over the years, looked over Franny professionally and found a dress that was exactly right. She had fair hair and blue eyes, she needed soft colours, the mauve and rose shades on this particular dress would just suit her. She also said that Franny must get the best haircut that could be afforded, and drove her into Thorpe Milton where it was done, and where she actually opened a bank account. That was a fortnight before the wedding.

Back in her old clothes, she helped Mrs. Grant decorate the church with Michaelmas daisies, asters and late white roses from the Mansfield Park gardens. Occasionally she looked at the memorial tablets, or the floor tombs which went back as far as the seventeenth century. Some of them were for very young people, a beloved daughter or son who had died at around her own age. She thought a great deal about poor Sylvie and about her mother's pain.

The wedding was on a perfect September afternoon. Tom, though still in disgrace, was allowed home for the weekend, and Eddy, who had already started his first job, came down from London for twenty-four hours. He said that Missy was singing in a charity concert and sent her love and apologies. It was true, but she had already decided not to be there because she didn't want Maria to be reminded of that unfortunate affair with her brother on this day of all days. There were a great many reporters and celebrities. Maria looked glamorous in pure white, Julia and the second bridesmaid a little less glamorous in pale violet. There was a reception in the big house, and on this occasion Franny was allowed to mingle with the visitors while waiters passed round the drinks. She could hardly take her eyes off Eddy, who only had time to exchange a few words with her.

Pictures of the happy couple appeared on several front pages next day.

13

Henry Crawford returns

For almost three months after the wedding Franny led an extremely quiet life, since none of her cousins were around. Tom was not welcome at Mansfield Park, Mr. and Mrs. Rushworth had returned from their honeymoon and moved into their Park Lane flat, Julia was back at Essex University and Eddy and Missy were living in the shared house off Seven Sisters Road. Sir Thomas, when he was at home, was quite affable, and she was deeply grateful to him for giving her an allowance and her own phone. There was plenty for her to do in the house and grounds but she was sometimes sent into Thorpe Milton on errands, and then she was able to get an odd hour in the library or wander around some shops.

One afternoon she spotted two girls, Kelly and Hayley, who had left school at the same time as herself. They were sitting in the window of an Italian ice cream parlour and gestured to her to come in. She hadn't thought they liked her, but soon she was chatting to them quite happily over a cappuccino and they were all catching up on their news. Hayley was working in the Co-op, Kelly training to be a hairdresser, and they each had a boyfriend.

'Have you got a job, Franny?'

'Well, I do the housework, and some of the gardening –'

'Are you going to ask us to your stately home?'

'I'd like to', Franny faltered, horribly embarrassed, 'but, you see, my aunt, Mrs. Norris –'

'I know all about her', Hayley broke in. 'My Gran lives in Mansfield village, and she's stopped going to church because Mrs. Norris is always nagging her. You can't do anything with a person like that'.

But she feared that they still believed she was a snob. And when the two boyfriends came in, and they all started shrieking and laughing together, she felt herself in the way and said, quite truthfully, that she must run for her train.

On a cold December morning Mrs. Grant, seeing her cutting holly for the Christmas decorations, invited her into the Parsonage and made her some hot chocolate. Dr Grant was upstairs, finishing his book about the Arian heresy, and was on no account to be disturbed.

'I can cook', Mrs. Grant said, passing a plate of mince pies, 'but I can't garden. I have a best friend who's a passionate landscape designer, but I was always more interested in people. Have you got any bright ideas, Franny?'

Franny was shy of giving an opinion to an older person, but she didn't feel nervous with Mrs. Grant. It was obvious that the Parsonage garden had been neglected for a long time; Mr. Norris and the clergyman who came after him hadn't touched it.

'Go on, tell me'.

'Perhaps you could ask your friend –'

'No, she and Theo don't get on and she hardly ever leaves Cornwall. What do *you* think?'

'Well', Franny said cautiously, 'you've got a yew tree, and that tall evergreen hedge, and a rosemary bush. You could plant some snowdrops and have a green and white winter garden'.

'Takes too long. And it isn't winter all the time'.

Franny looked out of the window and thought about it. The garden was quite small, although the house was a big one, in keeping with the days when clergymen had enormous families. And there were no children to run round it.

'I think, if I were you, I'd try a wildflower garden. If you get a good mix of seeds it could almost look after itself, and then it could attract butterflies, and bees, and hedgehogs. Eddy says the bees are actually in danger of becoming extinct'.

It was like an aching tooth, she thought. She would always love Eddy, and she would always think that Missy wasn't good enough for him, but there was absolutely nothing she could do about it so she would have to get used to it. And she would have to be careful not to drag his name into conversations, as she had done just now.

'Such a nice young man', Gillian said. 'I'm very fond of my sister, and she needs someone steady and sensible. She didn't have much of a home life. Now, I think the wild flowers are a very good idea. Perhaps we could drive out to a garden centre after Christmas and you could advise me'.

'I'd love that. Thank you very much'.

'Your spots are clearing up, Franny'.

'I know'. There had been a real improvement that autumn.

Her phone rang.

'I'm so sorry, Mrs. Grant', she said, after Mrs. Norris had harangued her for an entire minute. 'I'm needed at home'.

Parliament was in recess; Sir Thomas was back at Mansfield Park, and West Northamptonshire still hadn't selected a Conservative candidate. Henry had talked to a great many influential people that summer, and been quite confident, but since then he had spent most of his time in London. Now he had been warned that someone else was very interested: Dame Margaret Bullock, a single woman in her fifties who had had a long and distinguished career in local government. She lived in the constituency and several of the older members thought that she deserved it. It was time for him to come back, stay at the Parsonage and see whom he could charm.

Sir Thomas invited him for a quiet dinner. When he entertained at home he used a catering firm, and he was rather proud of his cellar. It was a very small party, in the breakfast room under the gaze of an earlier Sir Thomas in his wig, with only Lady Bertram, Mrs. Norris and Franny, who had put on the lovely dress she had worn at Maria's wedding. Henry politely stood up when she entered the room. Lady Bertram had been showing him a picture of the new Mr. and Mrs. Rushworth in *Hello* and he was looking suitably impressed.

When Gabriela brought in the port it was time for the gentlemen to talk politics, and the three females left the room.

'I am a little worried about it', Henry admitted. 'Of course, I'd like to see many more women in Parliament, but I honestly don't think Dame Margaret is the right person'.

Sir Thomas, who detested bossy women, agreed.

'I shall certainly do what I can for you, Henry. You may as well get around and – press the flesh, I think it's called – while you're staying with the Grants. And then there's the Huntingdon Ball; I hear that the tickets aren't selling. Perhaps you could go there with a suitable young lady'.

'I think I should do that', Henry said.

That evening, alone in his bedroom, he phoned Missy. They usually spoke two or three times a week, and first, he asked how Eddy was.

'Hard at work. He brings home huge piles of marking and sits up terribly late with it; I'm sure he'll soon get bored. We're still madly in love. How are *you*?'

'I take it that Eddy isn't listening?'

'No, he's gone for a run round the block. What exactly are you up to, Henry?'

'I wanted to ask you about that girl, Franny Price. Has she got a boyfriend, do you know?'

'I shouldn't think she's ever had one. What's it about?'

'I need someone to take to the Huntingdon Ball'.

'Surely no problem. You could take – what's her name? – Annabel'.

'I don't think Annabel would go down very well with the Tory matrons. Two of them actually asked me last time I was here if I was married or engaged. And it's not only the ball, I need to go about and make myself agreeable to the good people of Northamptonshire. Franny looks distinctly more attractive than she did in the summer. I was quite surprised'.

'You were running round with the Bertram girls and didn't notice her. No, leave Franny alone'.

'My dear girl, I'm not going to eat her. Actually she's quite a pretty little thing, and we could have quite a pleasant time'.

'Henry, do remember that she's very inexperienced'.

'Oh, I'm quite aware of that', Henry said.

14

Franny's First Date

Franny came in out of the winter afternoon in her gardening clothes to find Henry Crawford in the marble hall, chatting agreeably to Gabriela.

'Franny, I was hoping to catch you', he said. 'It so happens that I have tickets for tomorrow's matinee of Shakespeare's *Henry the Eighth*, in Northampton, and won't you come with me? It's going to be rather good. There are also a few friends that I'd like you to meet'.

'Well –'. Franny could hardly speak for surprise. 'Thank you very much'.

Lady Bertram appeared at the top of the staircase; she had been wondering when someone was going to make tea. She smiled down at them graciously.

'What a lovely idea'.

'But – aunt – will you need me –?'

'Not tomorrow afternoon, Franny, I'll be busy with Cynthia. Take her out by all means, Henry. Are you staying for tea?'

'No, thank you, Lady Bertram; I'm afraid I'm expected in town. So I'll call for you at half past one, Franny'.

He was gone leaving her absolutely stunned.

'Thomas, why is he taking *Franny* to the theatre? She's so stupid, he'll be embarrassed to be seen with her. I thought it was Julia he liked. Why hasn't Julia come home?'

Sir Thomas had had a busy day and would have liked to relax with his *Telegraph*. He thought, not for the first time, that his sister-in-law was an annoying woman.

'I should let the young people settle these things by themselves', he said.

Julia was more generous than Maria with her cast-off clothes. Most of them didn't fit Franny, because she was much smaller and slighter than her cousins, but she managed to get into a white cashmere jumper, nearly new, and a dark skirt of her own. She was shaking with nerves.

Mrs. Norris had worked herself up into a state. She stared balefully out of the window as they left the house and Franny knew there would be trouble when she came back. Henry ushered her into the front seat where Julia had sat on the trip to Sotherton. She had been very worried about being alone with him, but gradually relaxed on the drive as he chatted and she found that she wasn't expected to say very much. Had she been to the theatre before? Then it was high time she started. He had done a lot of amateur acting at Cambridge and he particularly loved Shakespeare. The Henry play wasn't often performed and he'd be interested to see what she thought of it. There were no awkward pauses. She could see why people thought he was charming; she just couldn't understand why he should be bothered with her.

The theatre was fairly full; Henry gave her a programme and a packet of chocolates. While she was still admiring the splendid red and gold decor, the curtain rose, and she soon found herself totally absorbed. She had done some Shakespeare at school, she was used to hearing blank verse and the acting was first-rate. She felt passionately sorry for poor Queen Katherine, middle-aged and plain and surrounded by all those self-seeking men. Henry glanced at her from time to time, and was pleased.

In the interval, a well-dressed couple aged around sixty came over and talked. They introduced themselves as Reg and Theresa Falconer and Franny learned that they were all going on to a wine and cheese party at their home.

'So this is Sir Thomas's niece,' Theresa said, sounding delighted, 'and I hear that your charming sister is going out with his son'.

'His second son. Yes, they're living in London, very happy'.

'Dare I say that Shakespeare is rather a bore – ', the man said.

'Reg, really!'

'The old boy certainly understood politics', Henry put in.

'My wife's the cultured person. Henry, did you know that the unspeakable Margaret – ?'

The talk became political. Franny understood very little, but soon they were back in their seats and she was struggling to hold back her tears at Queen Katherine's death scene. Then she was whisked back into the Jaguar and they were driving very fast through dark twisting lanes to the Falconers' house. It wasn't like Mansfield Park, of course, but it was warm and spacious, with a giant Christmas tree in the hall and a table spread with sparkling glass and silver, snacks and wine. Patience, a smiling middle-aged Zimbabwean lady, took her coat. She would have liked to talk to her, but a few minutes later people started coming in and she was being introduced.

Franny soon realised that she needn't have been nervous. The guests, most of whom were over fifty, were all very pleasant and did most of the talking; everyone already seemed to know that she was Sir Thomas's niece. There was only one awkward exchange, when an old lady in a fascinator pinned her against the wall and interrogated her.

'So why are you living at Mansfield Park, my dear child, instead of with your birth family?'

'Oh, well', Franny stammered, 'my mother is a single parent, and it was difficult –'

'And what does your father do?'

'He was in the Navy, but – well – we don't see much of him now'.

'Very sad. So the Bertrams kindly took you in –'

'– very kindly –'

' – to give you an education. Did you go to Cheltenham Ladies' College, or Roedean?'

'No, Thorpe Milton Upper'.

'*Where*?'

At this point she was thankful to find Henry by her side.

'Well, Henry, I see that you've been keeping the little cousin under wraps', boomed the old lady.

'She's not *my* little cousin. Excuse me, Lady Osborne, I'd like to introduce Franny to some more people'.

He steered her away and whispered to her to stay close. After that, she only had to smile and let the conversation flow round her. She gathered that this was a fundraising party and kept hearing about Dame Margaret, whom everyone seemed to detest. And then, quite suddenly, they all began to thank their hosts and leave. She also thanked them and then Henry took her arm and drew her away.

She had drunk a glass and a half of wine, much more than she was used to, and was feeling dazed, and worried about what was going to happen next. Mrs. Norris had warned her about girls who got drunk and accepted lifts after dark with strange men. But Henry drove the thirty miles back to Mansfield Park without stopping and then drew up with a flourish in front of the house. The moon was rising, and the urns and statues on the patio were glittering with frost.

He walked her politely to the main door.

'Thank you very much', Franny blurted out, just as she had done when she was a child.

Henry drew her into his arms and kissed her gently on the cheek. She almost panicked, but then, to her intense relief, he let her go, and she stumbled inside.

15

Franny's Flu

She had got through it, that was her main thought the next morning. She had had her first date and her first kiss, the only problem was that it had been with the wrong man. Eddy and Missy were expected home for Christmas and she dreaded seeing them together. But, although she still thought that Henry was rather plain, he had turned out to be much nicer than she had expected, and she was glad, too, that she had gone out in company and not disgraced herself.

She did disgrace herself that afternoon.

Mrs. Norris had appeared, after a busy morning running the Women's Institute in Thorpe Milton. It was obvious that she was angry, but so far she hadn't actually said anything. Sir Thomas was thinking mainly about his cactus collection, which he intended to rebuild, partly, too, about politics, but he had observed, in a grand and careless way, that Henry Crawford seemed interested in his niece, and he thought this was perfectly suitable. They were all having tea in the Yellow Room when Henry strolled in, warmly welcomed by the three adults.

'You left your programme behind, Franny. I do hope you had a pleasant time'.

'Oh, *yes*, thank you very much', Franny said gratefully. 'I did love the play'.

'That's good. And I wondered if I could take you to the Huntingdon Ball on New Year's Eve? I badly need a partner'.

Franny almost dropped the Wedgwood jug from which she was measuring milk.

'Thank you, but I can't – I've never actually gone to a ball – my aunt needs me –'.

'I can spare her for one evening', Lady Bertram said kindly.

'An excellent idea', Sir Thomas said.

'I can't', Franny said desperately. 'Please excuse me'.

'Don't worry', Henry said diplomatically, 'just let me know what you decide. No, I won't stay for tea. I'm at the Parsonage if I'm wanted'.

Mrs. Norris was already giving her vicious looks and, as soon as Henry was out of earshot, Sir Thomas let it be known that he was seriously displeased.

'Really, Franny, you are no longer a child. Your behaviour is embarrassing. You should be flattered that a man like Henry Crawford wants to take you out and you ought to be thinking about the Party, not yourself. It's important that he should become the next member for West Northamptonshire. I thought that all young women enjoyed going to balls –'

'She needn't think it's her that he wants', Mrs. Norris snapped. 'Julia – '

Lady Bertram said helpfully, 'She can have Julia's pale blue dress. I'll ask Cynthia to alter it'.

This time she really dropped the milk. She was having a panic attack, but she thought it was a heart attack; she couldn't breathe and there was a dreadful throbbing in her chest. It was worse than the worst times she had been bullied at school. She was clutching a chair to support herself but was terrified that she was going to fall down. She heard Lady Bertram give a slight scream and Sir Thomas ring the bell. At some point Gabriela rushed in, told them not to worry, got her upstairs and on to her bed and talked soothingly for several minutes as her breathing gradually returned to normal.

'What was it all about, Franny? That Norris, what will she do next? I like your new boyfriend. He is so attractive and sophisticated'. Gabriela was proud of her English. 'And they say he is going to be the next MP, perhaps he take you to live with him in London'.

Franny went on crying. She didn't want an attractive, sophisticated man, who was probably going to be the next MP; she wanted Eddy. And she could never have him. She could never compete with the Crawfords, who were so charming and assured and who invariably got their own way. A partner, she knew what that meant. She would have to go to the ball with Henry and she would be expected to sleep with him. Henry slipping out of Tom's party with Maria, only weeks before her wedding. Missy, who was going to marry Eddy – she knew that he was going to marry her. It was all much more than she could take.

Gabriela promised to keep everyone away and to bring her a supper tray, but when it came, she couldn't eat. She fretted about what the adults were going to say to her in the morning. She had a horrible night. She dreamed that she was walking down the aisle of Mansfield church to be married to Eddy when somebody got up and stopped the wedding, just like in *Jane Eyre*. The next thing she knew was that her throat was burning, the little clock said five past ten and Mrs. Norris was standing over her, demanding to know why she hadn't got up. She started to cough painfully and bring up thick yellow phlegm, and Mrs. Norris fled.

An hour later, the Bertrams' private doctor came in, took her temperature, and told her that she had 'flu. 'There'll be no Christmas parties this year, young lady; you should stay in bed for at least a week and probably longer', he said. He left instructions that she was to have a complete rest.

Franny fell back on the pillow, still weak but unspeakably thankful. She didn't know whether she had picked up a germ at the wine and cheese party, or if it was psychosomatic, but in any case, she hadn't got to do anything. For the next few days, she dreamed and dozed and read a little. Lady Bertram looked in once and said some kind words, but nobody else, except Gabriela, came near her. She heard voices and laughter from far below, as Sir Thomas hosted a sherry party, and was relieved not to be there. Very slowly, she began to sit up and feel more normal.

Two days before Christmas, Julia breezed in.

'Hi, Franny. Gabriela says you've been ill. How are you?'

'Much better, thank you', Franny croaked.

'If I were you, I'd stay up here. Norris is always on the warpath at Christmas and spoils it for everybody. Well, I just walked up from the station, and the first thing I saw was Henry's car. I was gutted. Gabriela says he's been staying at the Parsonage for some time'.

She doesn't know yet, Franny thought, and when she does she'll be angry.

'I'm terrified', Julia went on in tragic tones. 'I'm not a political person, but obviously, if they're going to choose between Henry and that gruesome old battleaxe, Dame Margaret, it's going to be a no-brainer. Which means he'll be in and out of the house plotting with Dad for years to come. I've tried very hard to be sensible, but if I see him, I'll want to go on seeing him'.

'I know', said Franny. She picked up *Jane Eyre* from the floor and read out the sentence which had particularly struck her: *A pleasure like what the thirst-perishing man might feel who knows the well to which he has crept is poisoned, yet stoops and drinks divine draughts nevertheless*'.

'Yes', Julia agreed, 'that's exactly it. I think it's high time I had a serious relationship. Maria's always had lots of admirers and now this brilliant marriage, not that I can personally stand Rush, and I've never had a proper boyfriend. She always overshadowed me at school and then uni. You can't think how awful it is, Franny, to have a sister'.

'I do have a sister. In Plymouth'.

'Oh, yes. I know that everyone's nasty about John Yates, but he does seem to like me. And I quite like him, but of course, he isn't Henry'.

Whether or not Julia had been told about Franny's theatre date, she didn't visit her again. Tom was nobody knew where, and Mr. and Mrs. Rushworth were on holiday in the south of France. But Eddy came home on Christmas Eve, with Missy, and as soon as they had greeted his parents they climbed upstairs to her attic room with a pile of presents.

'The liqueur chocolates are from Henry', Missy said. She was looking radiant. 'He likes you, you know, and he's so sorry you're ill. Did you have a good time at the play? Gill also sends her love. This is a flying visit, but if you hurry up and get well we can all go out, the four of us'.

Eddy was also looking very happy.

'They've been overworking you, Franny; you need a break. I'm glad Henry has taken you out. A nice chap though we don't agree about politics, he's almost one of the family now'.

It was agony.

She lay there after they had left, thinking that at least she had escaped from the Huntingdon Ball, and that as soon as Christmas and New Year were over she would get up and work out what to do next. She felt that she had offended Sir Thomas, who had been so kind to her, and she didn't want to see Mrs. Norris or any member of the Crawford family ever again. Nor did she want to see Eddy, if it kept reminding her of what she could never have. The Bertrams were not her birth family. She had reached this point when her phone rang, and it was her brother, William.

16

Franny in Plymouth

'Did you get my parcel, Franny?'

'Oh, yes, thank you so much. I'll open it tomorrow'.

'Your voice sounds peculiar'.

'I've got a cold. How are you all?'

It was two and a half years since she had seen William, and the eight years since she left Plymouth had changed him from a cheerful little boy into a strapping young man. Since leaving school he had worked his way around Europe doing various odd jobs. His ambition was to see the world.

'I've got brilliant news. VSO have accepted me; I'm going to dig a well at a village in Zimbabwe. Did you know, some people have to walk miles to fetch water, two hours there and back every day?'

'I know. I often think that we're very privileged'.

'I didn't get much warning, because someone else dropped out. I've been rushing round madly sorting things and I'm flying to Africa –'

'When?'

'January the fourth. Franny, can't you come down and see us before I go? I'm not sure when I'll get back, and it's been ages'.

'Oh, *yes*', Franny said. Everything in her was saying yes.

'Franny, are they treating you all right? You're very hoarse. I like Eddy, but all the other Bertrams are snobs. Those two girls looked right through me when I was at Mansfield. Come back and stay for a long time'.

She got up, feeling shaky but distinctly better, four days after Christmas. Gabriela had kept her up to date with the family news. Missy was officially staying at the Parsonage, but she and Eddy had spent nearly all their time together, and had borrowed Sir Thomas's car and taken it to Oxford for a weekend. They were now back in London, and Julia had gone away too, in her case without saying goodbye. Mrs. Norris had caught Franny's 'flu and was laid up, to everybody's relief, in her own house.

She timidly knocked on the door of Sir Thomas's study.

'I brought you a little cactus, uncle'.

'Ah! Thank you, my dear'. Sir Thomas was studying several specimens, all taller and grander than her own, on his screen. He looked tired and preoccupied.

'If I can be spared, I'd like to visit my family in Plymouth'. She explained about William.

'A very good idea', Sir Thomas said. 'Have you enough for your fare, Franny? Your allowance will be paid at the month's end as usual, with another hundred pounds as a Christmas present'.

He was not going to say anything about Henry Crawford. She felt a worm.

Breaking the news to Lady Bertram was more difficult, because, now that Franny had recovered, her aunt declared that she couldn't do without her. But for once her husband was quite brusque.

'Certainly Franny should go. Gabriela can look after you. Family ties are important, and it's very creditable that young Will wants to make himself useful in Africa'.

'Franny makes herself useful to *me*', Lady Bertram complained.

She travelled on New Year's Eve, much of the time standing in crowded carriages, from Mansfield to Northampton, then to Birmingham where she missed the connection and finally towards Plymouth. As the train moved west, she heard more and more voices talking in the Devon accents of her childhood. It would be wonderful to see her mother and the whole family after all these years, and perhaps they would want to keep her with them. Never to see Mrs. Norris again, or see Missy and Eddy together. By the time she got there, it had long been dark, and there was some sort of party going on in the station. She thought briefly about Henry, almost certainly now dancing with somebody else at the Huntingdon Ball.

William was waiting at the barrier, hugged her, took her case and got her onto a bus.

'Mum's longing to see you. She says she'll hardly know you, it's been eight years'.

After several stops, they got off and walked up a narrow street where she recognised some long-forgotten landmarks; the disused Methodist chapel and the Goat and Compasses inn where one of her stepfathers had spent a great deal of time. The house itself seemed surprisingly small. They stepped straight into the front room, and she looked round at once for her mother, but could only see two boys who were yelling loudly as they rushed up and downstairs.

'Susie!' shouted William.

A sulky-looking girl of fourteen stepped out of the tiny kitchen. Franny was introduced to her sister, Susan Porritt, and her brothers, Sam Porritt and Charles Groves, now twelve and nine. Charles had been a baby when she left home, and she wouldn't have known the other two.

'But where's Mother?'

'She's down the Goat', Sam said, 'they're having a New Year's party'.

'Franny, why are you talking posh?'

'Oh, shut up!' Susie snapped at the boys. 'Franny, I'm sure you want something to eat after your journey; I've got tea and baked beans. The little devils ate all the chocolate biscuits. You're going to share my room'.

The boys started tossing a football about.

William had moved his camp bed out of his brothers' room and into Susie's, and would sleep on the sofa for the next few nights. He soon left to meet his friends, saying they would talk properly in the morning. Franny, dazed, accepted the meal which her sister plonked in front of her, noticing that the knives and forks were not quite clean.

'Is Mother going to –?'

'She won't be back yet', Susie told her, 'she said plenty of time tomorrow. Come on, I'll take you round'. She showed her the bathroom, which had damp towels and underclothes scattered all over the floor. 'And this is our room while you're here'.

A small room, even smaller than the Mansfield Park attic, just space for two beds, a clothes rail, a rickety table and one chair.

She unpacked, washed and crawled into bed. She thought she could hear a great clock strike midnight, and then cheering as the revellers spilled out of the pub, but after that, nothing.

17

The Abode of Noise,
Disorder and Impropriety

New Year's Day. Somewhere a church bell was clanging. Franny woke up, remembered after a moment where she was, dressed and hurried downstairs. She found Susie making toast and a woman in a skimpy nightdress, who had to be her mother, eating breakfast on the sofa with eyes glued to the television.

'Franny!'

'Mother!'

They embraced. Susie turned the sound off and gave her a mug of tea.

'I'm so happy to see you'.

In fact she was shocked. Seeing her mother in the flesh, in full sunlight, was very different from glimpsing her briefly on Skype. She was obviously Lady Bertram's sister, but although she was three years younger she seemed older; she had certainly once been a pretty woman but the years hadn't been kind. She had not yet washed off last night's make-up and her hair was badly dyed, streaked with grey.

'Well', said Mrs. Price, lighting a cigarette, 'long time no see. How are my sisters, Fran? They never bother to ring me up. Susie, where's William?'

'He went out, Mum; he has heaps of last-minute things to do'.

'Your aunt Desiree, her that married the parson, has a wicked temper', her mother continued. 'She wouldn't speak to me for years, just because your Dad was rude to her once. And her ladyship, your aunt Maria – her daughter's got the same name – she's a snob'.

'I'm not a snob', Franny said, almost in tears.

'I see your Uncle Tom now and then on the box. Terrible about that girl, wasn't it? He's very rich, judging by that great house and that lake. Do you think he could do anything to give my boys a start in life?'

'I – don't know'.

'You might ask. Well, it's lovely to see you, Franny. Stay on a few weeks, you could be really useful. I've got the boys to get back to school, and their uniforms are in a state'.

It wasn't what she had expected.

William was always kind in the short time he was there. He took her and Susie to Plymouth Hoe, and bought them burgers and milk shakes, but he had multiple things to arrange before he left England and she could well understand why he wanted to go. And then there were the two little boys to get ready for school. She took piles of clothes to the launderette, ironed them and sewed on the buttons which had been ripped off. She was very anxious to make herself useful.

The house was dirty and smelled permanently of cigarette smoke. Mrs. Price spent hours doing her hair and nails and muddled through what was left of the day. Franny realised that she actually had a lot in common with Lady Bertram; she would have got on perfectly well if she had married somebody like Sir Thomas and had a dress allowance and a cleaning lady and a Romanian maid. Like her, she knew all the characters in the soaps and all about the A and B list celebrities, but she took very little interest in her sister's family or in Franny herself. If Mrs. Norris, on the other hand, had been a single mother, she would have forced the children to behave and have made sure that the household was properly run.

Just as in Lady Bertram's boudoir, the television was always switched on. It was on even when nobody was looking at it, and the boys had their own set in their bedroom and watched it far into the night. Franny found the noise almost unbearable. She had hoped to make friends with Sam and Charles, but they were not interested. They were forever racing through the house with their friends, shouting and demanding food, or running round the streets after dark, banging on doors. No effort was ever made to control them.

With William gone – that was a painful parting – she and Susie spent more time together. The spring term at her school had begun. Afterwards, Susie took herself to the public library and stayed there until it closed, came home to eat and then retreated to her room with her homework. But while they were undressing and after they were in bed they had some long talks.

'Mum's only interested in the boys. She wants me to leave school as soon as I'm allowed and get a job, probably in the Goat or a supermarket. But my teacher says that I'm university material'.

'Susie, of course you must go to university if you can'.

'Oh, I mean to. I'll worry about the fees later on. I want to be an economist'.

'Really?'

'I want to understand things. Credit crunches, and the balance of payments, and the pound and the Euro. I keep hearing about them, but I want to know what these things actually mean. I'm *never* going to live like Mum'.

Franny found that she was getting fond of her half-sister. At first she had been rather shocked by Susie's manners, but she could now see that it was natural for a bright girl, who had never had much attention at home, to struggle against the mess she lived in. She racked her brains, trying to think how she could help Susie.

They got into a routine. Franny found herself working quite as hard as she had done at Mansfield Park, cooking, shopping, tidying, trying to see that the kitchen and the horrible bathroom were kept clean. Before bed, make sure that the boys' lunch boxes were packed and their uniforms ready. In the morning, get them up, feed them and turn them out of the house, complaining loudly that they hated school. She now knew that they sometimes played truant and that the social services had visited her mother more than once.

Weekends were easier, and when everything was done she sometimes went by herself to the small local park and looked for the first signs of spring. It was understood that she was staying on until her birthday in February. No one had asked her to come back to Mansfield, but she supposed that Mr. Hawkins would want her to be there when the grounds needed attention. She found herself dreaming of the carpet of snowdrops under the beech trees, the peace and quiet in the great house when Mrs. Norris wasn't around. It made her dreadfully guilty to find that she wanted to get away from her own family.

One Saturday morning, after she had been there three weeks, Susie had set off for the library as usual and she was making the beds when her mother called up the stairs, sounding quite excited:

'Franny! There's a gentleman here to see you'.

She immediately thought of Eddy. She looked quickly at her reflection, took a minute to change into her nicest top and ran a comb through her hair. Then she almost rushed downstairs.

Henry Crawford was smiling at her.

18

Henry Crawford in Plymouth

'I had some business in the west country', Henry said, 'and couldn't resist calling. Thank you for letting me into your home, Mrs. Price. I met the rest of your family outside –'

The two boys burst through the front door.

'Franny, is that your boyfriend?'

'Mister, is that your Jag?'

'Can I have a ride in it?'

Franny experienced a thrill of horror, and of relief that she had at least pulled the curtains and cleared the breakfast table, but Henry seemed quite unperturbed.

'Can I have a *ride*? I'm begging you!'

Mrs. Price – who, thankfully, was fully dressed – said proudly, 'That's my Sam and Charles, aren't they fine little boys?'

'Indeed they are'.

'Would you like some Nescaff?'

'No, thank you, Mrs. Price, I've had breakfast, but may I take your daughter for a walk? And these young men perhaps could come for part of the way?'

The boys spilled out into the street, shrieking with excitement. Franny meekly followed; of course, it had been absurd to think that her visitor might have been Eddy. He was happy with Missy and his job and probably never thought of her. Henry got them all into the red Jaguar and drove expertly, and as if he knew where he was going, towards Plymouth Hoe. He parked and produced a ten pound note.

'Now, Sam, go and buy yourselves ice creams and then find your way home. I want to talk to your sister'.

They rushed off – not thanking him, Franny noted with distress – and, to her considerable amazement, she found herself walking along the Hoe by his side. It was a lovely day for late January. The water was deep blue, the sky almost cloudless. It crossed her mind that now Henry had met her family and seen the state of her mother's house, he would surely lose all interest in her, but somehow, that was not a welcome thought.

'I was so sorry to hear that you'd been ill'.

'Oh – thank you, but I'm much better'.

'You still look a little pale. I'm afraid, whether it's here or at Mansfield Park, you're overworked. My sister says you always get the jobs that no one else wants to do'.

'Have you seen your sister?'

'Yes, I looked in the other day on her and Eddy. They send their love. I don't think they're actually engaged yet but it seems probable'.

So it's settled, Franny thought.

'I wanted to say – I would have liked to see much more of you before Christmas, but you were unwell, and I had so much to do. You know I have ambitions to go into Parliament, and I've been very busy finding out about the constituency. *My* constituency, I'd like to say, but of course it isn't yet. People call us the nasty party, but that's not how I see it. I wonder, did you ever hear about the Scratton estate? It's one of those 'sixties tower blocks, probably a death trap in case of fire, children running wild, lifts not working and drug dealers openly pushing their stuff. I've talked to the people who have to live in places like that, and it shocked me. I'd like to be in a position to make a difference'.

It sounded so unlike the Henry Crawford she had thought she knew.

'Do you think I should try, Franny?'

'Oh, of course – you know it's right –'

'I intend to make a lot of changes if I get the chance. Meanwhile, I'm driving back to London this afternoon, and after that to Northants where I'll look more deeply into the problems of – well, 'my' constituents. I wonder if you're tired of Plymouth yet? I could take you back with me'.

'I can't', Franny said, trying to speak steadily. 'I've got responsibilities here. My sister –'

'Susie. I talked to her outside the house. She's a very intelligent girl'.

'I'd like to get her out of this'.

'Of course. I can see that you're devoted to your family'.

'I meant –'

She didn't know why she was saying this; Eddy wouldn't like it if he heard her discussing her family with an outsider. Only if he married Missy – and he would, she knew he would – Henry would be one of the family. She realised that he was standing quite close to her, but he did not touch her. His eyes were a very dark brown. He was not as plain as she had once thought, and he seemed so much kinder.

There was a pause, but not an awkward one, and then they walked a little further in the winter sunlight. Henry noticed that she was shivering and took her to a cafe for a mug of hot chocolate. He went on talking quietly, saying nothing to embarrass her but much that made her wonder if she hadn't misunderstood him. At last he drove her back to her front door and got out of the car.

'I'll have to go'. This time he didn't kiss her but took her hand in both his; they felt warm and strong. 'By the way, I told your mother a white lie; I haven't really got any business in Plymouth. I came here, of course, to see you'.

19

Mary Crawford Slumming

Ten p.m. on a foggy February Friday, in the neighbourhood of Seven Sisters Road.

Missy said a laughing goodnight at the little Greek restaurant, just round the corner from the house which she shared with Eddy and three other people. She had been waitressing there since before Christmas, a part-time, short-term job. She told everyone that she was an actress but was resting, and it was almost true. She was on the happiest of terms with the owners; they said they couldn't do without her and gave her leftover delicacies 'for you and your fiancé, Mary'. Several of the guests had asked her out, but she always refused. Her butterfly days were well and truly over. She was totally committed to Eddy.

And how ignorant she had been, she thought, as she let herself into the house that she'd never much liked, to think that teachers had an easy time. Eddy was pushed to the very limit. He knew the names and family backgrounds of all thirty-five children in his class. He worried about pupils who were being bullied, who couldn't speak English, whose mothers had criminal boyfriends. He was always being kept outside normal hours for breakfast club or after school club or staff meetings. And he brought home mountains of work. When she threw open his door, smiling, he was crouched at his desk marking a pile of books by lamplight, and hardly looked up.

'Hello there!'

'Hello', Eddy said abstractedly.

'Well, now I'm back, please put away those books and relax. It's Friday night, Eddy! I've brought you a half bottle of gorgeous Samos wine, and some little honey cakes'.

'Can't stop. If I'm going to take you out tomorrow, I'll have to get on'.

'We *must* go out. I thought of a trip down the river, and there's an open air play on Sunday afternoon, my best friend has a part, you'll love it. Do drink this'.

'Got to keep a clear head. Thank you, I will later'.

His phone rang. Missy felt the familiar wave of tiredness which always hit her at around this time.

'What an hour to ring! Well, I'll change into something more comfortable –'.

'Hello', Eddy was saying impatiently. 'Yes, Ed Bertram'. A male voice at the other end. 'John Yates? Where exactly are you? Has a doctor seen him? *What* happened? Well, don't leave him alone, for heaven's sake! I'll be there as soon as I can'.

He ended the connection and began to scramble through his smartphone.

'Tom's had an accident. He's in Newmarket with his friends; it seems he got drunk, fell down a flight of stairs and broke an arm. Missy, there's a train that I can just catch, I must go'.

'Oh, Eddy!' Missy was shocked, but felt this was exactly the sort of thing that Tom would do. 'Shall I pack you a bag?'

'No, sorry, there's no time. I'll ring you'.

She heard him rush downstairs and the front door being slammed. Her lovely weekend was in ruins. She kicked off her shoes, had a glass of the delicious wine and fell, too tired to think, into bed where she slept soundly for eight hours.

The train was overflowing with Friday night crowds. Eddy got a seat, but gave it up to a tired-looking woman who had just come off a cleaning shift. He rang his father, failed to reach him, and left messages at both his numbers; he had been worried about the estrangement from Tom, which had now lasted for six months, and thought this might be a chance to put things right. He rang Mansfield Park, but was told by Gabriela that Sir Thomas was not there and Mrs. Norris had gone back to her house. He changed at Cambridge, hung around some more, and eventually got out on the deserted platform at Newmarket. There was no barrier or ticket office; it felt like the middle of nowhere. He groped through some dark, nearly empty streets and found the right hotel. The bar had closed, but John Yates was sitting there by himself, drinking his way steadily through a pile of beer cans.

'Hi', he said, raising a languid hand. 'How's little Julia?'

'I haven't seen her lately. Where's Tom?'

'Oh, in room 12. Thing is, I've a gig tomorrow, and we've all got to be out by eleven, so could you look after him, Ed? Take him back to the stately home or wherever they'll have him'.

'Yes, I think I should. How is he?'

'Oh, they've set his arm, it's not serious. He says he just wants to sleep'.

Eddy spoke to the night porter and then went upstairs to the room where Tom lay. He was half dressed, one arm was in a sling and he clearly hadn't shaved for some time. When the light was switched on, he cursed.

'How are you feeling, Tom?'

'Shut up. Turn off that light. I've been through hell; I need to sleep'.

Not seeing what else to do, Eddy took off his shoes and jacket and lay down on the spare bed. It was hard to sleep. Throughout the night, he checked several times on his brother, who snored loudly but gave no other sign of life. At last a greyish light seeped through the curtains, and he got up and opened them. There was an agonised groan from the bed.

'Tom, I'll take you home'.

Tom gave a cry of pain and was violently sick.

20

Missy considers her Future

Missy woke at her usual early hour and remembered what was going on.

She found three messages from Eddy. The most recent said that he wasn't happy about Tom, and wouldn't allow him to be moved until a doctor had seen him. She got up and took a shower in the communal bathroom, but before she had quite finished, someone banged on the door. It had to be Baz, the least favourite of her housemates. She wrapped herself in her dressing gown and came out to find him on the landing, rubbing his eyes and wearing only a dirty singlet.

'Really, Baz!'

'I'm in a hurry'.

The man was a boor. Wrinkling her nose in distaste, she let him pass and went into the kitchen to make breakfast. Another housemate, Philippa, and her new boyfriend had brought back an Indian takeaway last night and left the containers and dirty plates lying about for someone else to clear up. She was beginning to dislike this place quite fiercely.

She took her coffee and croissant into her own room and wondered what to do, now that she was forced to spend the weekend without Eddy. She would practise for an hour on her harp, she thought, never mind if it annoyed Baz. She would see what Henry was doing. She would contact a few people who might be of use to her. It was still rather early to ring Eddy, but if only she could get her Equity card, and some work, the two of them could move out. When she was twenty-five and came into her inheritance, they could afford a nice flat. And surely, surely, he could give up teaching at the end of the school year and look for something more suitable. She knew that teachers were always leaving the profession, exhausted. They'd discussed it more than once, but so far, he had been very stubborn.

Eddy rang just after she was dressed.

'I knew you'd be awake – it's good to hear your voice. I finally got through to Dad, and he's coming down later with a specialist. Of course he feels terrible. I can't get any sense out of Tom. I asked him the Prime Minister's name, like you're supposed to do, and he just mumbled. Then I spoke to the man who picked him up after the fall. It seems that as well as breaking his arm, he hit his head'.

'Eddy, that's awful. Does your mother know?'

'She does now, I think; Norris is going to tell her'.

Anyone but Lady Bertram would have rushed to her son's bedside, but of course Eddy would be left to cope with everything.

'And the hotel is trying to throw us out, because there's a big event today, a wedding, and they want his room. I'm determined not to let him be moved before it's safe. Head injuries have got to be taken seriously. If –'

He broke off, almost choking. Missy thought, he's worried about brain damage.

'It's such a comfort to talk to you. I'll be in touch. Oh, just one other thing, Missy; it's Franny's birthday, and it would mean a lot to her to hear from you. Could you message her, please, and also let her know what's going on?'

'Of course. Do ring back soon, Eddy'.

'I will. I blame John Yates; Tom was all right till he got in with that crowd. I'll go now, but I'll keep you up to date'.

Missy found herself too worked up to touch her harp. She walked up and downstairs several times with her phone in her hand, observing the grubby wallpaper and broken banisters and wondering what she was doing in this run-down house, living next to people she had nothing in common with. She couldn't get seriously upset about Tom. After all, the accident had been his own fault, and it was months since she had stopped even mildly liking him. A thought flashed through her mind; what a pity that he's the elder son.

She stopped her restless walking, stared down at her phone which didn't ring. Did that mean that she actually wanted Tom to *die*?

Of course not.

Yet brain injuries, as everyone knew, were very serious, and she didn't suppose that anyone, even his parents, would miss him much after the first shock. It would completely alter Eddy's prospects. He'd be expected to help his father with the administration of the estate, which Tom had never done; he would have a good reason to give up teaching. And in course of time, he would inherit Mansfield Park and the cluster of farms that belonged to it. Sir Thomas was under sixty but wouldn't live forever, and the title would be inherited, too. 'Sir Edmund Bertram'. 'Sir Edmund and Lady Bertram'. 'Mary, Lady Bertram'. They sounded good. She saw herself, a favoured daughter-in-law, giving civilised parties in the gardens or the grand public rooms for her theatre friends. It wouldn't exactly help her career but wouldn't hurt it either. She thought about it for a long time, and almost forgot her promise to contact Franny.

Some hours later, Eddy rang again. Sir Thomas had cancelled his engagements and rushed to Newmarket. The doctor he had brought with him was not happy about Tom, and he was being moved to Addenbrookes Hospital.

MissMaryCrawford@happydays.com

Sad news

Hi, Franny!

Happy Birthday, and I hope you're having a lovely time with your family. It's good that you've reconnected after all these years. Henry said that he met them in Plymouth the other day and liked them all very much.

I'm afraid I have some rather dismal news. In case you haven't heard, Tom fell downstairs (while drunk!) at his hotel in Newmarket and is in intensive care; they think he may have fractured his skull. Sir Thomas is at his bedside and all is forgiven. Eddy, needless to say, had to rush off at dead of night and at the end of a week's work to deal with it. He is so kind and sensible that I can't help wishing we didn't have an absurd class system and that he could be the eldest son. 'Sir

Edmund' sounds nice, doesn't it? Still, only the good die young and I'm sure you needn't worry yourself about Tom. Hope to see you soon, in Mansfield or wherever and much love,

Missy.

She pressed the Send button, and then thought that perhaps she had been tactless; it almost sounded as if she wanted Tom out of the way. Still, she had only betrayed her thoughts to Franny, who didn't count.

21

Maria and Julia

'Maria'.
'Yes'.
'Could we drive over to Cambridge to see Tom?'
'No'.
'Why ever not?'
'There's no point, Julia. It isn't like an ordinary hospital visit. He's unconscious, wired to a machine; he wouldn't know us'.
'Do you think he might –?'
'I haven't the faintest idea. I hope he either dies or gets completely better; it's not worth surviving with brain damage'.
'That sounds cruel'.
'It's true'.
'Mummy seems remarkably calm about it'.
'You know what she's like. I really think her I.Q. is somewhere in the low seventies. Eddy and Dad think there's no need to upset her'.
'Well, if you won't take me, I suppose I can't go'.
Pause.
'Maria'.
'Yes'.

'Are you going to Jan Stornoway's party?'

'Not sure'.

'What relation are they to the Crawfords?'

'No relation. Jan's husband is the brother of Andrew Stornoway, who's the boyfriend of Missy's stepmother. He and Missy had an affair, which is why the stepmother threw her out'.

'Oh. Well, I came to London mainly because of this party – actually uni is a bore, I might not finish my degree. But I just spoke to Jan, and she said that Henry was going'.

'Henry Crawford?'

'Yes. First he was going to visit his constituency, and then he agreed to stay in London for a while. Maria, if he's going to be there, I can't go. I absolutely couldn't bear to be in the same room'.

'That's childish'.

'I couldn't go through all that again. Did you know that he took Franny to the theatre?'

'*Franny*?'

'Yes. They were all talking about it at Christmas. They think he's serious about her. And then she went to Plymouth to see her family, and he went after her'.

'Nonsense. Franny's only a teenager and a very plain one. He was probably just amusing himself, because you and I weren't around'.

'That's what Norris says, but it's exactly what I mean; amusing himself is all he ever does. Well, that's definite; I shan't go to this party'.

'I might'.

'Why, what for, after the way he treated you?'

'See if he thinks I care'.

'You're a married woman'.

'I don't feel like one, since Rush is forever training or touring or out with his friends. And even when he's at home he sits and stares at the box and has no conversation. Henry's amusing, at least'.

'Maria!'

'Have you had a good dose of his mother? We stayed with her at Sotherton for a week and it nearly killed me. She's as common as dirt and still thinks I'm not quite good enough for her adorable son'.

'Well, it's your funeral'. Julia got up from one of the two deep sofas upon which they had been reclining. 'I think you're playing with fire. I think I'm going to ring up John Yates'.

22

Franny and Joey

'I do think Mum ought to have remembered your birthday', Susie said. 'After all, she was *there*'.

Franny doubted whether very many people remembered it. Coming down on the Saturday morning that she turned nineteen she had found exactly two presents, a book token from Eddy and a parcel, containing three little ebony elephants, from William in Zimbabwe.

'Nothing from your boyfriend Henry'.

'He's *not* my boyfriend'.

'If you'd told me', Susie said, 'I'd have got you a card at least, but I've got literally no money'.

'I have'. Her allowance for February had come through as usual. 'Only I can't very well go on taking money from Uncle Thomas if I'm not doing anything. I ought to be thinking about going home'.

Susie looked so woebegone at this that Franny wished she hadn't said it.

'Never mind, I'll treat you. We'll go to the Marine Aquarium, just us'.

They didn't say anything to Mrs. Price or the boys about birthdays, just walked out into the sunny morning, and after they had spent two happy hours looking at the marvellous fishes had lunch in the cafe overlooking the sea. Susie, tucking into a strawberry ice cream, declared that this had been easily the best day of her life.

'Tell me some more about Mansfield Park, Franny'.

'Okay'. She told her about the Canaletto, and the gardens, the white marble hall and the large quiet rooms where you could retreat to read in peace. She was missing them desperately.

'So far as I can see, Mrs. Norris is the only fly in the ointment'.

'Yes, she is'.

'Is Lady Bertram *retarded*?'

'Oh, no, she's very kind'.

'Franny, I wish I could go back with you', Susie said. 'You know that Mum's got this new boyfriend, Joey'.

She had seen Joey, and didn't like him. That was the problem; when she returned to Northamptonshire, it was going to mean leaving Susie behind.

They wandered home in the late afternoon and found Joey and their mother watching football and in no mood to talk. Franny got the old PC working, with some difficulty, and looked for her messages. That was when she read Mary Crawford's e-mail and found out about the accident to Tom.

She cried out with shock.

Susie, who was reading over her shoulder, asked, 'Are you fond of Tom?'

'Yes – well, not specially, but it's a terrible thing to happen –'

'You're not in love with him, are you? Because people never ought to marry their cousins; it means that the children might be handicapped. I mean, disabled'.

Another shock.

'Are you sure?'

'Positive'. Susie was always positive. 'I know a girl whose parents want her to marry her cousin as soon as she's sixteen, and she's only fourteen now. I told her to talk to a teacher. You wouldn't do it, would you, Franny? It isn't because of Tom that you want to go back?'

Franny was silent. She had never heard this until just now, and it was upsetting. She would have to find out whether or not it was true. But of course, cousin or no cousin, she knew perfectly well that she would never stop loving Eddy.

As if that made any difference.

She re-read Missy's e-mail, and could clearly see what had been in her mind. The Crawfords were always lucky. Tom would die, and in course of time Eddy would become Sir Edmund, and he and his wife would inherit Mansfield Park. And Henry would probably become the member for the neighbouring constituency, and she would keep on bumping into the three of them for as long as they all lived.

'Franny, what *are* you thinking of?'

'I was only thinking about myself', Franny said. 'Tom's very ill. I might have to go back as soon as tomorrow, if I'm needed'.

She rang all the people she could think of. It was impossible to get through to Eddy, but she finally spoke to Lady Bertram, who said tranquilly that she wasn't worried; Tom only had a broken arm and his father was with him. She added on a plaintive note, 'When are you going to come home, Franny? I'm tired of having to do everything without you'.

Mrs. Norris snatched the phone from her sister.

'Really, Franny, why are you pestering us, and at such a time? You might not know the meaning of the word, but I'm extremely busy. We can manage perfectly well without you, thank you very much'.

Eddy finally rang her on Sunday night.

'I've taken leave from work. Someone has to be with Tom, and Dad had to go back to Westminster, but he'll pay whatever it takes for the best treatment. I never used to believe in private medicine but I can see the advantages now. It's horrible to see him wired to a machine; they're doing everything they can but they just don't know if he'll ever get better. No, stay on in Plymouth, Franny, enjoy your holiday, though of course you're upset. I'll ring again tomorrow'.

Tom on life support, Eddy with him day and night, frantic with worry, while Tom's mother, sisters and Mrs. Norris hadn't gone near him. Mrs. Price, too, seemed quite unconcerned. She hadn't seen Tom since he was a small child, and it was years since she had spoken to her middle sister.

And then there was her own family. She was obliged to see a good deal of Joey while the younger children were at school, since he hadn't a job. He and her mother spent most of their time watching television, doing the lottery or chatting, usually about celebrity romances or characters from the soaps; Lady Bertram could happily have joined in the conversation if she had been there. He was a small man with bad teeth and dyed orange hair. His breath smelled; he was dirty and coarse. They talked about him moving in and she profoundly hoped that it wouldn't happen before she went home.

One day, about a week after Tom's accident, she had come back from the launderette with a basket of clean sheets to find Joey reading the paper. For once, he was the first to speak to her.

'Hey, Fran, is that girl Maria Rushworth your cousin?'

'Yes, she is'.

'And is that Henry Crawford a friend of yours?'

'Well –'

'Just look!'

Appalled, Franny read the proffered front page:

RUSH AND MARIA SPLIT

'The Toff and the Tough'

Maria Rushworth has sensationally walked out on her husband, just six months after they wed.

She has eloped with 28-year-old barrister and man about town Henry Crawford (right). A friend said, 'Maria knows now that she made a terrible mistake. She and Henry are deeply in love and have something very special'.

Maria's father is Tory MP Sir Thomas Bertram, of Mansfield Park, Northamptonshire, where singer Sylvie Stratton-Booth tragically drowned in August. His office declined to comment.

The pair are thought to be hiding out at Henry's £250,000 thatched cottage in Everingham, Norfolk (below). Neighbours said they had seen them in the off-licence buying olives and champagne and that they 'seemed very fond of each other'.

Mrs. Elizabeth Rushworth said last night, 'I never liked that girl. She never had any affection for my son James, she was just after his money that he made by his own efforts. This Mr. Crawford better watch out; she's got a nasty temper'.

BREAKING NEWS: The West Northamptonshire Conservative Association has confirmed that Mr. Crawford is not their candidate.

So it was to be Dame Margaret after all.

23

Return to Mansfield Park

Eddy sat in the Intensive Care Unit beside Tom's bed and watched the red and green lines zigzagging up and down on the screen. His brother's eyes didn't open; there was no sign that he would ever wake again. He was too tired to think; it was days since he had had an uninterrupted night's sleep. Every so often they turned him out so that a doctor or nurse could attend to Tom and then he grabbed a meal in the canteen, or dozed in a chair, or rang his family with the latest news and again apologised to his head teacher for his absence from work. Sir Thomas had come down twice, obviously anguished, but there was nothing he could do, except repeat that he was prepared to pay whatever it took; the House of Commons, where he served on several committees, required his presence.

Tom, who usually never stopped talking, had retreated into a great silence, and Eddy was trying to get his head around the possibility that he might die. The doctors hadn't ruled it out. But people of his age weren't supposed to die, although one of his schoolmates had been killed in a skiing accident, and there had been Sylvie. He still winced at the thought of what her mother had said. But then he had hardly known either of them, they were not his brother.

One afternoon, in the visitors' room to which he had been banished, a kind woman gave him a cup of coffee from the machine and yesterday's newspaper. The liaison between his sister and Henry Crawford was splashed all over the front page.

Franny was horribly distressed. She had been there when Maria stood up in church, only six months ago, and promised to devote her life to James Rushworth for richer for poorer, in sickness and in health, forsaking all others, for as long as they both lived. Of course, she saw now, Maria hadn't taken it seriously. She had wanted to have a fairytale wedding and to be famous, and had got her wish.

And Henry, who had really seemed to like her? She wasn't in love with him, so why was she so upset?

She couldn't get it out of her mind; she felt worse and worse as she tried to make sense of it. The story was in all the tabloids, they got a new angle on it every day, although really there was nothing to add. She thought of Sir Thomas, already desperately worried about his elder son, how he would hate having his family name all over the gutter press for the second time in a year. And poor Eddy, who wasn't even allowed to get on with the job he loved, he too would hate the publicity.

Mrs. Price and Joey were quite excited to read a story about people they actually knew.

'I'd have thought she'd stick with Rush', Joey said, 'he's the one with money'.

'No', her mother said, 'Henry's obviously not poor, and he's got lovely manners. It's just a shame he didn't pick our Franny'.

She could hardly bear it.

One afternoon when her mother had gone out and Franny was making tea, Susie came home in her P.E. outfit. When she took off her mackintosh, Joey leered at her.

'Good pair of legs you've got, Sue. Why don't you walk round the house wearing nothing?'

'I'll kill him', Susie said between her teeth as soon as they were upstairs.

Franny decided that she needed to stop worrying about the Bertrams and do something about the looming crisis in her own family. It wasn't her mother, she now realised, whom Joey was interested in. It was Susie.

Next day, she went out, turned on her phone, and sheltered from the cold wind in the closed doorway of the Goat and Compasses. She knew she had got to talk to a responsible adult, but she didn't like to contact her uncle or Eddy when they were in so much distress about Tom. She had just decided, reluctantly, that Mrs. Norris was the most suitable person, when the phone rang, and it was Mrs. Norris herself.

'Gabriela's getting married', she said furiously. 'She told me, with no warning whatever, that she proposes to leave us and live in Thorpe with this man and never wants to see us again. Of course she's only doing it to get a British passport. And to walk out when we're in so much trouble! You'll have to come back at once, Franny. You've had a fine time in Plymouth, enjoying yourself as you always do, but I shall have a heart attack if this goes on. My head is splitting'.

Franny had never heard her aunt admit to any human weakness before.

'Can I bring my sister?'

'Who?'

'My sister, Susie'.

'How old is she?'

'Fourteen'.

'Yes, you may. Mind, I shall expect her to pull her weight'.

'Yes, of course, aunt, but she'll need to go to school'.

'That's no excuse. She can make herself useful outside school hours, and so can you. I want you here *now*, Franny, or tomorrow at latest'.

Luckily it was the February half term holiday. Franny checked her bank balance, and found they could afford to get the coach to London and the train from Euston. She told Susie to pack as much as she could carry and they set off next morning in high glee. She was sorry to leave her mother, and the little brothers she had never got to know, but the sad truth was that the gap between them had grown wider over the years and she could find no way across it. Mrs. Price herself seemed quite resigned to waving them off.

'Now, remember', she warned Susie when they were aboard, 'do everything that Norris says, and be very polite to her'.

'I'm not frightened of cross old women'.

'I want you to stay on at Mansfield Park, and get your GCSEs'.

'Oh, I shall'.

Their journey took practically the whole day. As they passed through London, they picked up a free newspaper and read, on an inside page but in banner headlines:

MARIA AND HENRY: 'IT'S OVER'

The whirlwind romance between Maria Rushworth and Tory hopeful Henry Crawford has ended – after just one week.

Neighbours in the village of Everingham, Norfolk, said they had heard a blazing row and saw the pair drive away in separate cars from the £300,000 cottage where they had been staying..

Rush's lawyers confirmed that he is seeking a divorce.

Henry Crawford was spotted last night putting out rubbish near his Chelsea flat. He said, smiling, 'It's all been very exaggerated. Mrs. Rushworth is a good friend, but I'm single'.

There was a rather good photograph of Henry putting out the rubbish.

'And I thought', Susie said, 'that he was such a nice man'.

24

Maria, I'll never stop saying

The two girls tumbled out at the deserted Mansfield station on a black, starry night. Franny unlocked the park gates and they walked the half mile up the drive, lugging their cases. It was too dark to see much, except the outlines of some trees, but she thought that hundreds of crocuses must be out by now. They staggered through the front door and Susan gazed in awe at the Canaletto and the marble staircase. Both their aunts were sitting in the Yellow Room and heard them come in.

Lady Bertram heaved herself off the sofa and embraced them.

'Dear Franny, now I shall be comfortable! And this is your little sister? What's her name?'

'Susan', Mrs. Norris snapped. 'Franny, get me a glass of Madeira. I'm worn to a frazzle, doing things for other people'.

Franny obeyed.

'And I must say, if you'd given that man Crawford a little encouragement, letting him take you to that ball when he kindly invited you, we might never have had this dreadful scandal. And when Tom is so ill, too!'

'Oh, I think he'll be better soon', Lady Bertram said soothingly. 'Thomas says they're doing everything they can'.

'You can believe that if you want. Well' – Mrs. Norris emptied her glass and slapped it down – 'I'm going to go back to my little house and have an early night and hope that I won't be found dead in the morning. Franny, you're in charge'.

All of them relaxed when they heard the front door slam.

'I do find Desiree a little trying', Lady Bertram said. 'She's so full of energy, which I suppose is a good thing. What do you think, Franny, Julia says she's not going to take her degree but is going to join the John Yates Four as a singer. Thomas doesn't like him, but he is an Honourable, after all, and he's always been polite to me. I never went to university and it did me no harm'.

No, Franny thought, Sir Thomas wouldn't like it, but she hadn't got the energy to worry about Julia's future. As soon as her aunt had returned to her costume drama, she took Susie up to the top floor and made a bed for her in Gabriela's old room. That was enough activity for one day. Her last thought before she sank into sleep was that Lady Bertram hadn't bothered to ask anything about Mrs. Price, her sister.

In the morning, there was plenty to do. She sorted out her old school uniform and made arrangements for Susie to attend Thorpe Milton Upper. She tackled a pile of dirty dishes and laundry and made sure that there was enough food in the house. In the middle of the day Mrs. Norris walked in, grey-faced and still complaining of a headache. She was just preparing some tea and aspirins when a very smart car swept up the drive and Maria, with a pile of monogrammed cases, got out.

She waited as long as possible before returning with her tray to the Yellow Room where Maria was holding forth to her mother and aunt while Susie, round-eyed, drank in every word.

'Just see if I care. That man's a rat, a viper. I never want to see him again, he hasn't got an elementary sense of decency. Who's that girl?'

'Your cousin, Susie'.

'Oh. Well, Franny, you needn't think that Henry Crawford liked *you*; he'll run after anything with two legs and a skirt. I'll never stop saying it, he's a callous monster'.

'Couldn't you go back to Rush?' Lady Bertram asked helpfully.

'No chance', Maria said with a hollow laugh. 'He's being incredibly vindictive and says I won't get a penny, but I'm going to keep the car, it's in my name. I've had it with Rush and I couldn't care less'.

'Nobody made you marry him', said Mrs. Norris. 'Your father spent a small fortune on your wedding'.

'How was I to know? There were three of us in that marriage – me, Rush and his mother. And how was I to know that those reptiles, those so-called gentlemen of the press, were going to follow me and Henry around? They were sitting on the wall at Everingham taking pictures. He didn't like it'. She burst into tears.

Franny, who thought this conversation unsuitable for Susie's ears, put down the tray and guided her out of the house. In the grounds, they found Mr. Hawkins, who was delighted to see her and said she had come back just in time for the daffodils, and that Mrs. Norris had given him a terrible two months. They made plans about the gardens.

That night, Sir Thomas rang to say that he was coming home for twenty-four hours. He hadn't been at Mansfield for a while, because there was still great concern about Tom, but he had constituency business which couldn't be put off and asked Franny to be ready to feed and water a group of visitors.

He spent the morning in his surgery at Thorpe Milton and drove up to the house at midday. Franny almost didn't recognise the elderly man who quietly let himself through the front door; he looked ten years older than at Christmas. He didn't want to talk very much but said to Maria:

'Couldn't you stay in one of your husband's homes for the time being?'

'He's changed the locks. I'm here because I've nowhere else to go'.

'This is very embarrassing for me'.

Maria didn't answer.

In the afternoon, some people drove up and spent three hours with Sir Thomas. Franny recognised Reg Falconer, whom she had met at the performance of *Henry the Eighth*. She brought them coffee and biscuits when they came in, and later tea and fruit cake. When her uncle reappeared he refused to discuss the scandal. Mrs. Norris, in particular, seemed to get on his nerves.

A taxi was booked to take him back to London at noon the next day. Before that, Franny nerved herself to knock on his door.

'Uncle, I know you've got a lot on your mind –'

'That's all right, Franny'. He was staring at a half bottle of Bristol Cream sherry and the little flowering cactus on his desk. 'I appreciate you running the house in the absence of domestic help'.

It was in both their minds that Franny wouldn't run away with a man, Franny would always be here.

'It's just that I'd like your permission to keep my sister with me'. She explained about Susie. 'I honestly don't think that she's safe in my mother's house'.

'I see', Sir Thomas said, reviving a little after a sip or two. 'Perhaps I should run a check on this man. What's his name?'

'I only know him as Joey'.

'Well, obviously you can't leave a young girl in moral danger. By all means keep her with us'.

'Would it be all right – if she went to school in Thorpe, and then to uni? She wouldn't expect any special favours; I mean, she'll help around the house, and take care of her own fees'.

'If she's capable'. He was considering what to do about Julia. 'Yes, I'd certainly encourage her to work hard and make something of herself'.

'That's really, really kind of you, Uncle Thomas'.

'You're a good girl, Franny'.

25

Missy speaks

The next two weeks were perhaps the most cheerful she had ever spent at Mansfield Park. She was out in the grounds most of the day, cutting the first crop of grass and delighting in the first signs of spring. Susie was thrilled to be here and they had long talks before bed every night. She had known all about Mrs. Norris from the first, but Lady Bertram astonished her.

'Doesn't that woman ever do *anything*?'

'No. It's just the way she is'.

'Just think if Mum had been like that, we'd all have been taken into care!'

The news of Tom was better. He had been moved into a nursing home in Cambridge, and was to be allowed home in the week before Easter. Sir Thomas had arranged a day and night nurse. He had also, though Franny didn't know this, taken steps to deal with the Julia situation. He told her that he couldn't stop her having a relationship with John Yates, much as he disliked it, but unless she immediately went back to Essex and worked for a degree her allowance would be stopped. Julia had sulked but complied. There was hope that she wouldn't mess up her life.

Maria also sulked, and made a great many phone calls, and sometimes drove up to London in her smart car.

All his children except Eddy, Franny thought as she deadheaded the daffodils and made plans for Susie's future, had caused him a great deal of grief. She had not seen Eddy for three months.

She hadn't seen the Grants either; they seemed to spend a lot of time away, although Mrs. Grant once waved as she drove past with another woman. It was embarrassing.

The day came when Tom was brought home, accompanied by his father and Eddy. They had been warned that he might never completely recover, but he walked through the door without support and spoke to them quite sensibly. But he was very nervous, and refused to go upstairs, so Franny made a bed for him in the former butler's pantry on the ground floor. Mrs. Norris annoyed him, so did his mother and Maria. The only companion he wanted was Eddy, who, as the school was closed for Easter, stayed on.

'Dad, you don't understand. Missy and I are unofficially engaged'.

Sir Thomas sighed; he had known this was going to be difficult.

'You are too young to get married, Edmund. I recommend a cooling-off period. I was nearly thirty when I married your mother, and you are only –'

'Twenty-three, but I know what I'm doing'.

Sir Thomas sighed again.

'As I said, I have nothing against the young woman personally, but her brother has involved our family in a most deplorable scandal. I always like to go to Sunday services when I'm here, but I simply can't face meeting the Grants after this. At least Reg Falconer tells me that Crawford is definitely not going be their candidate. For the second time in six months, the newspapers –'

'Dad, Missy has nothing to do with all this. She was afraid you'd react this way; she didn't come down with me because she thought you wouldn't like to see her. We aren't getting married just yet, and when we do the tabloids will have moved on to something else. It isn't the scandal that matters, it's Tom'.

Eddy wandered through the marble hall and checked on Tom, who didn't seem to want him at present. The nurse was young and cheerful and was telling him that he would soon get used to walking up and downstairs. He was sure that his father would come round eventually; there had been no embarrassing headlines for some time. The scandal would flare up again when Rush got his divorce and then, hopefully, his family would be left alone. He wanted to talk to Missy. He reached for his pocket, remembered with annoyance that he had left his phone in London, then moved on and found Franny in the scullery arranging some early tulips in a jar.

They hugged affectionately.

'It's so good to see you again, Franny. We haven't talked for ages. And I'm glad that you're keeping Susie at Mansfield Park; she seems a bright little girl'.

'She is', Franny said proudly. 'She says she's going to be an economist'.

'Good idea. There are plenty of intelligent children in my class and I'm encouraging them to get all the qualifications they can. I know I'm in the right job. I'm really looking forward to going back after Easter; the Head's been very patient, but I felt awful about missing half the spring term. I never liked to leave Tom because I was always afraid that it might be the last time. It's been hard on Missy, only seeing me sporadically, but she's been wonderful. She's kept busy with her harp and the Greek restaurant and she thinks she may have got a small part in a play. I must tell her –'

Her phone, which had been lying on the stone slab, rang.

'Hi, Franny', said Missy. 'I know you're at Mansfield. How's Tom?'

'He's much better, thank you. I'll just –'

She was in the act of passing the phone to Eddy.

'Oh!' Missy's voice, clear and beautifully modulated, echoed round the tiny room. 'Oh, well, there goes my chance of ever being Lady Bertram. Tough luck; I'd have quite enjoyed being the mistress of Mansfield. Is Eddy around?'

'He's –'

Eddy had gone a dreadful colour and let the phone slip through his fingers.

After a moment he said in an unnatural voice, 'She wanted Tom to die!

26

The End of Mrs. Norris

Eddy had rushed back to London an hour later, giving an excuse of some sort.

Nothing happened in the next few days, except that Mr. Hawkins announced that he wanted to retire. He would stay until a new gardener had been found, but he was over seventy now and couldn't have managed for as long as he had without Franny. Then, the night before he was due to return to Westminster, Sir Thomas called everyone together, except Susie and Tom, and told them that from now on things were going to be different.

'Does that mean that you're standing down, Dad?' asked Maria.

'No, I am not, Maria; I still have a great deal of public work to do. But before I go, I wish to put our home affairs in order. First, I think that you should leave this house as soon as possible'.

'Are you *turning me out*?'

'Not in the sense you mean, no, but I think it high time that you found a home of your own and a job. I may add that I was most hurt when you allowed Tom to go ahead with that deplorable party –'

'So I'm to have no fun at all?'

'You've had your fun, Maria, and you've exposed your family to some deeply unpleasant publicity. For the second time. In six months'.

'It's all Franny's fault', Mrs. Norris suddenly screamed.

'Desiree, really!'

'It is! If she'd gone out with that Henry Crawford as you wanted, he'd have kept away from Maria'.

'That's not true', Maria said indignantly.

'Don't interrupt me. You can't turn Maria out in the cold, she's your daughter, and this one is only a niece. You never should have let that girl into the house. She's sly and scheming. I've held my tongue for years' – her listeners were too astounded to comment – 'but now I'm going to say what I really think! She's brought her sister here, who's as bad as she is, and it's going to end with the Price family getting your money –'

Tom opened the door, with his nurse coming after him in distress.

'Can't you stop her? She's giving me a headache'.

'Calm yourself, Desiree', Sir Thomas said. 'Everything is all right, Tom. Thank you, Miss – yes, my son needs to rest, please return him to bed. Now', he added as the door closed, 'may we have a civilised discussion?'

But Mrs. Norris was not going to calm down. She raged about how Franny was idle and selfish, how all the recent disasters had been her fault, how she had let that girl Sylvie drown and allowed Henry Crawford to break up Maria's marriage. After a minute Franny fled to her attic, hoping that Susie was too far away to hear. Lady Bertram continued to look mildly surprised. Mrs. Norris picked up a Wedgwood cup and saucer and smashed them. Then she got hold of a crystal vase of daffodils, emptied it, and hurled it against the nearest wall, where it broke. Tom's nurse came back and asked whether she could help.

Sir Thomas very deliberately picked up his phone.

Mrs. Norris was given a sedative and taken to the John Clare Hospital in Thorpe Milton, where she was certified. Nobody was sorry to see her go. Even Maria, her favourite, only shrugged and said, 'I always thought she was mad'.

There was hope that she might improve in time. Meanwhile, Maria stayed on, complaining bitterly, and Julia did not return for Easter. Presumably she was somewhere with John Yates.

On the evening of Good Friday Eddy, white-faced and unshaven, walked in. It was only for a few days before the start of the summer term. He let it be known that he and Missy had broken up, and he didn't want to talk about it, but he did eventually talk to Franny, as they took a long walk with the Afghan hounds around the park.

'I suppose it's for the best. You see, I was so much in love with her that I ignored the warning signs, and there were plenty of them, actually. She really did want to get rid of Tom so that I could be a landowner and a baronet. Which never interested me'.

'That's cruel', Franny said.

'No, no, she isn't cruel, just – I suppose the best word is superficial. She never accepted, you see, that I'm committed to being a teacher. She kept suggesting I should give it up and look round for a directorship or something. And then there's the Henry business. She wasn't upset about him and Maria. I never liked Rush, but I draw the line at breaking up a marriage. And that reminds me –'

He walked on aimlessly for a short time, watching the squirrels running up the beeches that were beginning to break into leaf, going over it again and again.

'I don't think I shall ever get married. These last few days have been agonising; it was just as painful for her as for me. We were both crying. I offered to be the one to go, but she says she always hated the house, so I've got out of her way. She's going to move in with friends, or perhaps her stepmother. That woman was a bad influence. Missy is a lovely person at heart, but her brother and the people she grew up with –'.

He was silent for another five minutes, while Franny quietly padded behind him, before saying soberly:

'I shall never feel the same about anyone else'.

Sir Thomas delayed his return to Parliament while he got through some essential business, and then told his family that Mrs. Norris was not coming back. The doctors suspected a long-standing mental illness. She could perhaps be released after a few weeks, but he would no longer tolerate her presence at Mansfield.

'She won't starve', he said dryly. 'I am prepared to put a roof over her head, preferably a long way from here, but I shall find a couple who can take on the housekeeping and gardening, and can live at the lodge. Please don't argue. I now believe that I made a grave mistake by allowing her to have any share in the upbringing of my children'.

'Well, we were at boarding school half the time', Maria remarked. 'It was my friends, really, who brought up me and Julia'.

'Oh, dear', said Lady Bertram, adding after a moment, 'She's my sister, but she makes me tired. I think I'd get on better with a good housekeeper'.

Sir Thomas sighed. He was aware that many men of his age, including members of Parliament, divorced their first wives and linked up with younger women. But that was not his style.

27

Mrs. Grant steps in

Susie was enjoying school. Unlike Franny, she soon made several friends at Thorpe Milton Upper, and boldly asked if she could bring them home. Her aunt made no objection, and they all had tea and watched videos and romped up and down the grand staircase shrieking with laughter. Her teachers liked her, her homework was done well and regularly and she did her share around the house.

And Tom was slowly getting better. There was no question of him going back to his old way of life; he was still nervous and irritable, but he liked to walk around the park with the dogs and to spend his evenings playing video games. The nurse was no longer needed. Sir Thomas was hopeful that he would stay at home for good and eventually become his land agent.

None of this could have been achieved if Mr. and Mrs. Glazier hadn't moved into the lodge. They were a friendly middle-aged couple whose children had left home and who were happy to live in the country. Mrs. Glazier was an efficient housekeeper; her husband did the gardening and occasional driving. Mrs. Norris's belongings were tidied into black bags, moved out and stored in a garage. That had to mean that there was no chance of her ever coming back.

When William returned from Zimbabwe, full of his experiences, Sir Thomas invited him to spend a few days at Mansfield Park. He approved of a young man who did something for himself, more than could have been expected from his background, and they talked about jobs with the United Nations. This was at the end of May, and Eddy also came home for half term. He had been working very hard, seemed exhausted, and usually got up around midday and avoided people. Sir Thomas, who thought he had given up Missy reluctantly and out of respect for his family, considerately left him alone.

On the morning that William left, Franny and Susie walked with him as far as the station. He was going back to Plymouth and making plans. Joey was no longer around, to the girls' great relief, but his mother's way of life was still chaotic and he approved of his sisters remaining where they were.

'You've fallen on your feet, Franny', he said cheerfully. 'The stately home is a good place to be without old Norris. You could stay here for the rest of your life'.

When they had waved him off, and let themselves back in through the iron gates, Susie ran ahead and Franny followed more slowly, counting up the jobs that she still had to do. There was weeding, and sweeping up the hawthorn petals; she thought she would stay out of doors for a while to avoid Lady Bertram's pointless chit-chat. She almost didn't see Mrs. Grant at the parsonage window, waving vigorously.

'Franny, just the person I wanted to see! Come on in'.

In the garden, where the long grass was in a deplorable state, they relaxed at the ancient wooden picnic table over coffee.

'Now, first my news', Gillian said. 'I know it's been embarrassing for your uncle to have us on his doorstep, but we won't be here much longer. Theo is going to be the Professor of Church History at London University. Quite right too, he's wanted a job like that for years and he knows more about the fourth century than any other living person. So in a matter of weeks, we'll be off'.

'I'll miss you', Franny said, 'you've been awfully kind to me'.

'Missy is going to live with us. She was very cut up about Eddy, though she won't say so, and hasn't found another boyfriend yet. All those young people were getting on so well and it ended so badly. One never knows'.

'No, indeed'.

'Of course, Maria shouldn't have got married. I thought at the time that she seemed unenthusiastic. I'm not defending Henry – he's behaved badly, but I always think of him as the little boy who used to hide behind my skirts when he'd been stealing sweets. He had the most enchanting smile. All he wanted was a few days' fun, while Maria's husband was away, but unfortunately she took it very seriously'.

'She did. She's terribly upset'.

'But what I wanted to say, Franny, is that he talked to me for a long time about you. He likes you, you know. He likes you much better than Maria, but in the end, he thought you were too young and innocent'.

Franny felt tears prick her eyes.

'And you liked him a little, didn't you?'

'Yes', Franny admitted. She could say it now. 'Yes, I liked him, but I'm in love with someone else and I always shall be. It's no good, because he told me that he's never going to get married'.

'I've heard that one before. Now, Franny, before I go away – and obviously I didn't like to walk up to the big house after all that's been happening –'

'No, better not. Maria is still there'.

'I'm going to give you some advice. You're a legal adult – how old?'

'Nineteen'.

'And I think that it's time you got out. Those two women have made a slave of you, from what I hear, ever since you were nine. Lady Bertram is even worse than Mrs. Norris because she's a grown woman who expects to be cared for like a baby. You could go on in the same way, running round waiting on her, until one of you dies. You've got no friends of your own age; I don't count your cousins. Sir Thomas, much as I respect him, has obviously given no thought to your future. Mansfield Park isn't the right place for you now'.

'But –'

'Have another slice', Mrs. Grant said, indicating the raspberry sponge cake. 'You remember my friend, Olivia, whom I mentioned last time you were here? We've kept in touch ever since our schooldays. She runs a garden centre at a little place in Cornwall; her rhododendrons and azaleas are quite famous, and you may have seen her on TV talking about lost gardens. But even though she's a workaholic, it's getting too much for her. She's divorced and her children are not interested. She'd take you on, give you a room in the house, pay you and train you'.

'But she doesn't know me!'

'I've told her that you're a nice, quiet, responsible girl who likes gardening. That's good enough for her and after a few years, if you put your mind to it, you'll know almost as much as she does. You could become a landscape gardener, doing work you love. This is your chance, Franny, and it might not come again'.

'You mean that I should go away – live in Cornwall –'

'Not so far from Plymouth. You could visit your family at weekends'.

'But there's Susie. She isn't grown up yet'.

'Susie will be fine. She's a tougher girl than you ever were, and my spies tell me that everyone at the big house is fond of her. You can ring her every day'.

'Yes, Susie's got her own phone'.

'Think about it, Franny'.

She walked back towards the house, thinking that the white and purple rhododendrons on the long drive were looking as glorious as they had on that May evening when Mrs. Norris had brought her to Mansfield Park, all those years ago.

Rhododendrons and azaleas.

She thought about it, she continued to think for hours, and the only arguments against it seemed to be her responsibility for her young sister, and the likelihood that if she returned to the west country, she wouldn't see Eddy for years. He had always come home regularly, but he was unlikely to travel all the way to Cornwall just to see her. Well, perhaps that would be best. Perhaps in a few years he would bring his future wife to Mansfield to meet his family, and then she certainly wouldn't want to be here.

The first person she told was Susie, on the understanding that it was still a secret.

'Of course you should go', Susie said. 'You love mucking about in gardens, and I can visit you from time to time, though I wouldn't want a job like that myself. I've told Uncle Thomas that I'm going to be an economist. He seems to think that's very funny, but he's encouraged me to work hard at school. No, of *course* you don't have to worry about me. I'd ring you up anyway if I had problems. But they're definitely going to let me stay on; they like me'.

Yes, Franny thought; her sister was happy and doing well, and Sir Thomas and Lady Bertram probably liked Susie better than they had ever liked herself. But there was one more person she had to speak to before she made her decision; Eddy was returning to London next day, and in the morning there wouldn't be time.

He might encourage her to go. In that case she would know that he wouldn't miss her.

He wasn't in for supper. He had been wandering around the park with the Afghan hounds, and came in when it was nearly dark. Lady Bertram sat with them for a while, flipping through her magazine, and at half past ten yawned and left for bed.

Franny braced herself to speak.

'I've been walking about for hours', Eddy said abruptly as soon as they were alone, 'thinking. These last few months, I've learned a lot about myself'.

'I've got to tell you something', Franny blurted out, interrupting him for the first time in her life. 'I've been offered a job – a long way away, in Cornwall –'

'Franny', her cousin exclaimed, also interrupting, 'you can't leave Mansfield! I've got something important to say'.

28

Franny's Future

'I know it's a complete shock to you', Eddy apologised. 'Well, it's a shock to me, too. I've known you all these years – I've always been very fond of you, of course, but I somehow never thought of you in that way until now. Anybody would have been dazzled by Missy. She's so lovely – and charming – but I should have seen from the start that we weren't suited. Remember that time in Sotherton chapel when she was laughing about teachers? She liked me but she wanted to change me into a different person – someone who makes a lot of money and goes to parties – and then there was that horrible business about Tom. I ought to have known'.

He had grasped both her hands and was talking feverishly.

'You and I aren't like that. We've grown up together, we've got the same values and ideals. I know you only thought of me as a cousin, and perhaps you were fond of Henry – he's very like her, charming and superficial –'

Should she tell him that she had been in love with him half her life?

'I'm talking about marriage, Franny. We can be happy together – quietly happy. We can look after my parents as they get older, and they'll be delighted – they can't imagine Mansfield Park without you'. She had a vision of herself looking after an eighty-year-old Lady Bertram when she was fifty. 'You're not like Missy; you respect my job'.

'Oh, I do'.

He hadn't asked her anything about *her* job.

He was hugging her, kissing her cheeks and hair, and she knew that she should be overjoyed. This was the scene she had imagined for years, the man she had said only hours ago that she would never stop loving, and now it was all actually happening, and it didn't feel right.

She gently pushed him back, but went on holding his hands.

'Eddy, are you sure that you really mean this? You aren't on the rebound?'

'Of course not. I'm actually being sensible, because, as I'm sure you agree, Missy and I could never have had a happy marriage. I'm going back tomorrow – a staff meeting, but I had to talk to you, and you can get used to the idea, can't you, Franny? I can come back at weekends, and you can come to London. We'll speak every day. And then there's the summer, and we can spend all our time together. Yes, I'm sorry, I know it's a great surprise, but I seriously do mean it'.

Franny got very little sleep that night.

She had told Eddy that yes, she was surprised, but he knew how fond of him she was, and he must get some sleep if he was going to leave Mansfield and get back into harness next day. She kept asking herself what was wrong with her and why she had suddenly grown so cold and practical. The arguments bounced to and fro in her head.

I never expected this.

It's what I've always dreamed of, and now I can have it.

He's the nicest person I know.

He's probably the nicest person I'll ever know.

I'm only nineteen.

He's my cousin.

He knew me first, but he preferred Missy.

He's still obsessed with her.

He wasn't interested in hearing about Cornwall.

She considered all these facts.

In the morning she got up, heavy-eyed, and had breakfast with everyone except Lady Bertram, who took it in bed. There was no chance to talk properly, but Eddy kept looking at her and hugged her especially hard when it was time to say goodbye. Sir Thomas scooped him and Susie into his car, to drop her at school and him in London. The house fell silent.

She spent the next hour reading everything she could about gardens in Cornwall until it was a reasonable time to call on people. As she passed Lady Bertram's door, her aunt called out:

'Franny, can you find my reading glasses? I know I had them a minute ago. And take away my tray'.

Franny did so. Then she quietly went out of the front door and walked across the park in the direction of the Parsonage.

Eddy would be all right. He had the work he loved, and he would do it well even if he was unhappy for a short time. She would write to him – a proper letter, not an e-mail – and tell him that she would always love him, but didn't think that cousins should get involved in a closer relationship.

She hoped that he would stay friends with Susie and William. One day he would probably meet a woman who looked and spoke a little like Missy, but who respected his deep commitment to the children he taught.

The Grants' kitchen smelled of bacon, toast and kippers; the Doctor enjoyed a full English breakfast. He greeted her absent-mindedly and then retreated upstairs.

'I've been thinking', Franny said. 'I'm truly grateful, Mrs. Grant, and please may I talk to your friend Olivia –?'

'Olivia Freshfield. You'll get on'.

She dialled a number, spoke for a few minutes, handed her the phone and a cheerful voice said:

'Tell me about yourself, Franny'.

Epilogue

Franny walked down the drive with her luggage, towards the locked gates that opened on to the outside world. Alone, because her uncle was back at Westminster, Susie was at school and Lady Bertram hadn't yet got up. It was a beautiful June day.

Sir Thomas had put a thousand pounds in her bank account. He approved of what she was doing, and had said, 'I think you may have had – ah, a lot to put up with over the years'. Lady Bertram had been less amenable.

'I shan't be at all comfortable without Franny. She knows the way I like things done'.

'My dear', said Sir Thomas, rather testily, 'you have Mrs. Glazier to run the house, and Susie is perfectly willing to fetch and carry. Only I insist that the girl is allowed to complete her education. Franny didn't'.

She was going on a long journey. She didn't yet know that Henry would become a successful barrister but never get the parliamentary seat he craved; that Missy would have several admirers but none she liked as much as she had liked Eddy; that Susie would win a place at Murray Edwards College; that Mrs. Norris would go to a cottage far away in Yorkshire because there was nowhere else for her to go; that Tom would find he preferred a quiet life in the country; that Maria would get a job on a fashion magazine and Julia would hang round the fringes of the pop world until she met some more interesting men than John Yates. All this was in the future. Staggering under the weight of her luggage and her past, Franny walked away from Mansfield Park.